What if...
Your Past Came Back
to Haunt You

a choose
your destiny
NOVEL

What if...
Your Past Came Back to Haunt You

LIZ RUCKDESCHEL AND SARA JAMES

DELACORTE PRESS

Published by Delacorte Press
an imprint of Random House Children's Books
a division of Random House, Inc.
New York

Visit us on the Web! www.randomhouse.com/teens

Educators and librarians, for a variety of teaching tools, visit us at
www.randomhouse.com/teachers

Library of Congress Cataloging-in-Publication Data
is available upon request.

ISBN: 978-0-385-73643-5 (tr. pbk.)
ISBN: 978-0-375-89129-8 (e-book)

Printed in the United States of America

10 9 8 7 6 5 4 3 2 1

First Edition

GOODNESS GRACIOUS

Sweetness comes in many forms, but it's usually best when mixed with spice.

"What's this?" Haley Miller gasped in an exaggerated tone, moving aside to let her next-door neighbors, the Highlands, into the house. Barbara Highland was carrying a foil-covered pie in each hand, and notes of cinnamon, toasted pecans and caramelized apples wafted through the air in her wake. "I can't believe my nose," Haley added with mock outrage. "Joan Miller allowing processed sugar to darken her doorway? I never thought I'd see the day!"

"Very funny." Joan smirked. "Don't worry, the

sugar ban is lifted on holidays," she assured Mrs. Highland.

Barbara was followed closely by her doting husband, Oliver, and their very smart and very crushable son, Reese. A junior like Haley, Reese was captain of the soccer and track teams and was on the short list to be next year's class president, prom king and valedictorian. Haley suddenly remembered she was still wearing her long auburn hair in a messy ponytail and quickly yanked out the elastic. She then turned and gave Reese a not-too-eager hello that, while making it clear he was on her turf now, was still casual and welcoming.

Today was Thanksgiving, after all. That morning, Mrs. Highland had called in a panic to say that their oven was on the fritz and their turkey still raw and cold. Naturally, the Millers had invited the Highlands to share in their bounty. Joan and Perry Miller then roasted not one but two free-range turkeys and prepared a spread of organic vegetables; Barbara Highland would provide pies and other desserts, which, luckily, she had prepared the night before, pre—oven fiasco.

"Happy Thanksgiving!" Barbara said brightly. "It smells wonderful in here!"

Haley took a chilly cherry cobbler from Reese's hands and set it on the back of the stove to warm. Reese trailed her, looking over her shoulder somewhat suspiciously at the array of baked winter squash and pan-fried brussels sprouts. "Guess this means no candied yams with mini-marshmallows and canned whipped cream?" he asked.

Haley shook her head. "We do have gluten-free apple cake," she offered. "And Mom's special pumpkin pudding. It's sweetened with cane juice instead of sugar and tastes . . . earthy."

"Mmmm, earthy," Reese replied, feigning enthusiasm.

"You should count yourself lucky," Haley warned. "One year, Mom decided to 'experiment' by serving a braised tofu mold in the shape of a bird."

"Youch." Reese grimaced, then laughed.

Haley was glad they were clicking. She'd known Reese for over a year now, and had felt very close to him at times, but still wasn't totally convinced he shared certain sentiments. Even during their most revealing exchanges, Reese always held a part of himself back. Sometimes it seemed as if Haley had to get to know him all over again each time they were together. She loved the idea of spending Thanksgiving with the Highlands, but at the same time, all this cozy intimacy made her nervous. How would Reese behave tomorrow? Or the following Monday back at school?

"Well, I for one am anti-tofu on Thanksgiving," Reese announced. "Could you imagine the pilgrims and Indians sitting down to a meal of seitan protein and green tea powder? Being vegan is *not* what this holiday is all about."

Haley sensed her opening. "So tell me, who brought the marshmallows and aerosol whipped cream to the first Thanksgiving—was it the pilgrims or the Indians?"

Reese smiled sheepishly as Haley handed him a stack of plates. "Come on, help me set the table," she said, locking eyes with him. "You can tell me all about how the Wampanoag invented spray cheese."

"You jest, Miller, but cans of that stuff appear in cave drawings not far from Plymouth Rock."

Haley could hardly believe she had been dreading Thanksgiving this year. Just yesterday, her best-case scenario had been a moderately moist pile of white and dark meat laden with unlumpy gravy, followed by the usual fuss over her seven-year-old brother, Mitchell, who would undoubtedly be sucking up all the attention in the room or robotically disassembling whatever piece of electronics he could get his pudgy little fingers on. Haley's grandmother Gam Polly had decided to skip the festivities this year in favor of a trip to Barbados with her new boyfriend, Harvey Pickleman, so not even Gam would be there to lift Haley's spirits.

But suddenly, things were looking up. Like, way up. In fact, this was quite possibly the most fun Haley had ever had setting the table.

"Dinner's almost ready," Joan called out as the Miller-Highland crew filed into the dining room. Mitchell buzzed down the stairs dressed in a smallish navy blazer and one of Perry's old wide flowered ties, picking up a serving spoon to use as his mike and proclaiming, "Welcome to a Very Miller Thanksgiving Feast. Tonight's guests are . . . Reese Highland! Mr. Highland! The lovely and talented Mrs. Highland! And your hosts, the Miller family, starring me, Mitchell Miller! Yay! Yay!" He ran around the table making his own crowd noises.

"Don't mind him. He's been on this talk-show-host trip lately," Haley explained to a bemused Reese. "His role models tend to be your Mervs and Mike Douglases, the nineteen seventies guys, but once in a while he'll go off on a Letterman kick."

"Thank you, Mitchell," Barbara Highland said indulgently, "for the excellent introduction."

Joan took her place at the table and grabbed a wooden serving spoon. "Mitchell, let's try not to pester our guests." She was about to dive into the mashed potatoes with olive oil and rosemary when Mr. Highland interrupted.

"Shall we say a holiday grace?" Oliver asked, and Barbara and Reese bowed their heads in unison. Joan frowned, her spoon in midair. Haley worried for a moment that her mother might object to this suggestion. Prayer was not common in the Miller household, even on holidays. It wasn't that Haley's parents had ruled out the existence of a higher power. But they had both been undergrad science majors, and they still saw enough beauty in Darwin and nature to feel spiritually satisfied. The Millers also shared a mutual distrust of organized religion's collection plates, blind logic and shaming tactics. Nevertheless, Haley and Mitchell had been taught to respect their friends' and neighbors' and family members' beliefs and never to stand in the way of anyone's chosen traditions.

"Um, s-sure," Perry stammered. "Oliver, why don't you do the honors." Joan seemed okay with this solution.

"Thank you, Lord, for blessing us with this food. We thank you for always providing for our needs. And we thank Joan and Barbara for their hard work in preparing this meal for us today." Joan cleared her throat sternly, and Haley knew exactly what her mother was thinking. In the Miller household, chores were shared. Perry had done just as much as Joan in cooking the Thanksgiving dinner and therefore deserved just as much credit. "We ask that you bless this food for our bodies and nourish our souls. And we thank you, Father, for each person sitting around this table today. Remind us each of all the many things you've made possible on this Thanksgiving. In God's name we pray, Amen."

There was a brief moment of silence before Mitchell belted out the coda, "Through the lips, over the gums; look out, stomach, here it comes!"

Haley giggled while Perry rolled his eyes.

"Amen to that," Reese said, tousling Mitchell's hair before piling a heaping portion of cranberry-and-organic-sausage stuffing on his plate. Haley breathed a sigh of relief. Her family had successfully navigated a potentially sticky situation without compromising their beliefs or denying the Highlands theirs. The moment had also offered a clearer glimpse into Reese's family life. Maybe this was a key to understanding some of Reese's more baffling quirks.

"Perry, how's that little tree movie of yours coming along?" Oliver Highland asked as Haley's father began to carve turkey number one. Haley shot her dad a wary glance, sensing that this time, for sure, fireworks were on the way. Perry Miller was a documentary filmmaker who taught at Columbia. He was generally mild-mannered and even-tempered, but he took his work very seriously. His most recent film was an exhaustive study of the life cycle of deciduous trees in North America, which had taken years to make. Haley didn't think he'd enjoy hearing it referred to as "that little tree movie," especially by Mr. Highland, an investment banker. But a predinner beer had clearly had calming effects, because instead of blowing up, Haley's dad just nodded and said, "The tree movie's all done, thanks for asking. We're screening it at Columbia next week, as a matter of fact. Now all my free time is devoted to transferring the old Miller home movies to digital with a local post house. Actually, one of the assistants I'm working with goes to school with Haley and Reese. You two know a kid by the name of Garrett Noll?"

"The skater dude?" Reese asked. "He's a pretty cool guy."

Great, Haley thought, *the Troll now has access to the entire library of Haley Miller embarrassing moments. No wonder he's been giving me those weird looks at school.* She made a mental note to have a talk with her dad about just what footage was leaving the house.

"As far as your documentary work goes, what do you think you'll take on next?" Mrs. Highland asked, seeming genuinely curious.

"Well, my next film's still in the planning stages," Perry said. "I'm applying for funding now. But the topic is migration. Specifically, how global warming is affecting the migratory patterns of birds. Joan's work inspired the idea." Perry smiled across the table at his wife.

"Fascinating," Mr. Highland said, though Haley detected the slightest hint of a stifled yawn.

"I'll have to do some traveling for footage of the birds' habitats," Perry said. "Probably after Christmas, down to the mid-Atlantic states, maybe over into West Virginia. It's about time we got the family back in the car, right, kids?"

Haley nearly choked on her brussels sprouts. Her parents had been making noises for the past couple weeks about a possible upcoming road trip. Haley had assumed they just meant a jaunt up to Gam Polly's farm. But New Jersey to Appalachia in the backseat with Mitchell? This was not a journey Haley could handle, and it certainly wasn't her idea of a fun way to spend Christmas break.

"Uh, I may have to sit this one out," Haley said, racking her brain for a viable excuse. "Midterms are right around then. And you know how closely colleges look at junior-year grades."

"You could stay with us, dear," Mrs. Highland offered. "I'm sure Reese would appreciate having a study partner."

Haley blushed and used her napkin to wipe her face so that Reese wouldn't notice. "Sure, whatever's easiest."

"I didn't realize that birds were changing their migratory patterns, Perry," Mrs. Highland added. "I hate to think of not seeing my hummingbirds or thrushes at our feeders in the summer."

Joan shifted uncomfortably in her chair. Haley guessed it was because Mrs. Highland had just used the possessive in reference to wild creatures—just the sort of worldview that made Joan Miller crazy. "Migration is just the beginning," Haley's mother warned. "We could lose fifteen percent of all plant species in the next twenty years if we don't stop the strip mining and deforestation. It's all interdependent—the birds, insects, plants." Haley was glad Joan left it at that. As an environmental lawyer and activist, Joan often seized moments like these to break out a slide show, charticles and graphs. She was a good match for Perry, but when they got into one of their famously heated arguments, you wouldn't have guessed it.

Mrs. Highland shook her head and clucked, "That's just awful."

Haley watched as her mother tried and failed to stop herself from saying, "Well, it doesn't help when people like Eleanor Eton get swept into office."

Reese and Haley knew Eleanor's son Spencer, who dated the junior-class princess, Coco De Clerq. Haley was no fan of Eleanor Eton's political views, but watching Spencer and Coco—well, mostly Coco—lap up the attention surrounding the governor was entertaining, if a little disgusting at times. Judging by the VOTE ETON signs that had been posted in the Highlands' yard all fall, the Millers' neighbors fell on a different side of the party line.

"I don't know that Eleanor's such a bad choice," Oliver Highland offered. "I liked some of her thoughts on education. She seems able and willing to take criticism and hear suggestions. And it will be nice to see a woman running the state." Mr. Highland turned and looked fondly at his wife, and in that split second, Joan softened. She finished the rest of the meal politely talking gardening with Barbara.

"I saw Spencer at the mall yesterday, trying to shake off his mother's secret service goons," Haley told Reese in a low voice. "It was pretty hilarious. Who knows what he was up to, but those guards wouldn't let him out of their sight." Given Spencer's past antics, Haley guessed it was probably something illegal—perhaps a little gambling mixed in with some underage drinking. He hadn't been kicked out of three boarding schools for nothing.

"Yeah, I think those guards are there less to protect him than to protect Mrs. Eton's reputation," Reese whispered back.

"What are you two muttering about over there?" Joan asked.

"They're gossiping about Spencer," Mitchell reported from the seat to Haley's left. "Tell us more, Haley. Our viewers want to know all the dirt." She rewarded him by stepping on his foot. "Ow. Don't hurt me, Haley."

"Don't be such a bigmouth, then." Haley stood up. "More stuffing, anyone?"

"I'd love another slice of turkey, dear," Mr. Highland said. "Dark meat, please."

"I'll have some more green beans," Reese said, holding out his plate.

Haley refilled everyone's plates, then took her seat.

"How are you two handling all this junior-year craziness?" Perry asked the Highlands. "Haley's calmed down a lot, but I think the stress gets to me more than it does her."

"Getting into college wasn't easy when we were kids," Joan added. "But I don't remember being quite so busy all the time. Every minute taken up with activities and sports and committees . . ."

"I know what you mean," Barbara Highland said. "We were allowed to be kids in those days. We were allowed to have lives."

"We have lives," Reese said.

"I know you do, honey," Barbara said. "But I'm still amazed at the way you fit so much into a day." She turned to Haley's parents. "Soccer's finally winding down, so I thought he'd get a little break before basketball starts, but no, he's filling up the free time with the history club and the Spanish club and the Student Senate and Math Olympics and all these other extracurriculars. . . ."

Haley looked at Reese in surprise. She'd kind of thought the same thing—that once the soccer season was over, Reese would have more time to spend with his friends and, well, her for a change. This was the first she'd heard of the history club and all that. She could totally relate to the college pressures, beefing up the transcript, punching up the application. Good schools were hypercompetitive, and she wanted to get in as badly as anyone. But Joan and Barbara had a point—when was Haley supposed to have a life?

"Leave the boy alone, Barb," Mr. Highland said. "He's got a chance to go all the way to the top—Ivy League, whatever he wants. Now is not the time to stop and smell the roses. He can do that while he's at Princeton."

Joan, perhaps sensing a little family tension, pushed her chair away from the table. "I'm stuffed. Shall we take a little break before dessert? I'll make some coffee." She disappeared into the kitchen, followed by Perry.

"I think I'll check on the football game," Mr. Highland said, heading into the den. His wife joined him.

Haley heard Barbara whisper, "Honey, are you sure they have a TV? I thought maybe they were against it, you know, like the way they're so picky about their food."

"I just hope he doesn't want to change the channel," Mitchell said.

"Oh, Mitchell," Haley said. "Did you take apart the remote again?"

"I can't help it," Mitchell said, his eyes taking on that familiar crazy, feverish look. "It's just so much fun."

"Well, go put it back together. Now," Haley commanded. She got up and started clearing away plates. Reese helped her.

"So—the history club?" Haley said to him. "Student Senate? Math Olympics? How are you going to fit all that into your schedule?"

"It can be done," Reese said. "This is the year that counts, Haley. You said that yourself."

"I know," Haley said, but she still felt a little bruised by the news. From the day the Millers had moved to Hillsdale, New Jersey, there'd been something between Haley and Reese—an attraction and a bond—but their relationship never seemed to reach its full potential. Something was always in the way, whether it was another girl for Reese, another boy for Haley, a misunderstanding or now just their crazy schedules.

"My calendar's nothing compared to some people's," Reese said. "Look at Dave Metzger. Look at Annie Armstrong."

He was right, of course. Reese wasn't the only one trying to cram as much as he could into each day. Almost everyone Haley knew at school was going crazy with SAT prep classes and honors courses. Perry Miller was right when he said Haley had calmed down, but it seemed she was the only one at Hillsdale High School who wasn't in total college-panic mode. The place was frenetic. Annie Armstrong, debate team leader and Reese's main competition for valedictorian, had started four new clubs at school this year alone, including Planet Please, an environmental club whose goal was "to reduce our carbon footprint while marching to Washington." Membership was extremely time-consuming, involving picketing, protesting, fund-raising, letter-writing and schoolwide consciousness-raising.

"Annie doesn't count," Haley said. "She's not a

person, she's a machine. She's a computer with legs and a soap box."

Reese chuckled and took a pile of plates into the kitchen. At the mere mention of Annie, Haley found herself thinking about the debate team, and those thoughts led her, of course, to Alex Martin. Pesky thoughts. She tried to swat them away—*not while Reese is here!*—but they kept coming back, nagging at her like a mosquito.

She pushed through the kitchen door, dirty plates in hand, the image of Alex fiercely debating her in her mind. Alex was a senior, so he had the worst of the precollege grind behind him. Not that anything had ever been hard for him. Supersmart, very competitive and bookishly adorable, he'd shown more than an academic interest in Haley all fall. But he was so conservative, even more than Reese's parents. Politically speaking, Alex and Haley were like oil and water. Wouldn't it be dangerous to try to mix them? Wasn't that always a hopeless combination?

Still, she couldn't deny an attraction to him. How else could she explain the way he kept popping into her mind while gorgeous Reese was right in front of her?

Barbara Highland left the den and wandered into the kitchen to help with the coffee. "I brought my digital camera," she said. "Wouldn't it be nice to get some pictures of our families together?"

"That's a lovely idea," Joan said. "Kids! Let's gather in front of the fireplace."

"Um, where did you *leave* your digital camera?" Haley asked. Haley and Joan exchanged a knowing look.

"In the living room. Why?"

Haley dashed in that direction, and a moment later screamed, "Mitchell!"

"My camera! It's all over the floor!" Barbara exclaimed when she entered the room.

"I'll find him," Haley said. She checked the den, but he wasn't there. "Mitchell!" Haley shouted again, running upstairs to check his room. There he was, sitting on his bed, just putting the finishing touches on the reconfigured remote. "You're not supposed to take apart things that belong to guests—you know that!"

"I was bored," he said. "And the camera was sitting right there on the coffee table. . . . It was so tempting. You know how it is. A digital camera to me is like an electronic cupcake."

"Go fix it," Haley said. "Mrs. Highland is totally freaking."

She dragged her little brother downstairs. "We're so sorry, Barbara," Joan was saying as Barbara and Oliver continued to stare in shock at the remains of her camera. "But I promise it's not as bad as it looks. Mitchell does this all the time. And ninety-five percent of the time, things still work after he puts them back together."

"It's true," Mitchell said, sitting down on the rug to reassemble the camera as easily as if he were doing a toddler's wooden puzzle. The Highlands watched in amazement.

"That's incredible," Barbara gasped.

"Your son's very . . . different, isn't he?" Oliver said, less amused.

"He'll be done by the time dessert's ready," Perry assured them. "And we can take pictures then."

He herded the Highlands away from Mitchell's busy little fingers. Haley knew from experience that Mitchell would be able to put the camera back together as good as new, if not better. But watching him do it was often pretty nerve-wracking.

Unfortunately for Haley, all this fuss about cameras triggered thoughts of another classmate, Devon McKnight. Devon was a talented and serious photographer, friends with artsy rebels Irene Chen and Shaun Willkommen, and very cute in an unconventional way. He and Haley had been circling each other ever since he arrived at Hillsdale, and she still couldn't help finding him intriguing. Devon was quiet, moody and a little mysterious, which only made Haley obsess over him all the more. And no one could ever accuse him of overscheduling his time. He was serious about art, but not so serious about school.

"What'll you have, Haley?" Reese's blue eyes twinkled under his mussed black hair as he offered her pecan pie, apple pie, cherry cobbler, chocolate cake or her mom's pumpkin pudding.

What am I doing? she thought, chastising herself. *Look at the guy standing right in front of me offering me my choice of homemade desserts. He's nice, well-mannered, an athletic and academic superstar and the best-looking guy in our class. So why am I thinking about someone else?*

"I'll take . . . " Haley weighed her options carefully, then caught a glimpse of her mother's hopeful face. "The pumpkin pudding," she said finally, much to Reese's surprise.

"Are you sure?" he asked. Reese had tied Joan's apron over his jeans and button-down shirt to serve, half as a joke. It somehow set off his muscular shoulders and only made him more adorable.

Adorable, but not quite attainable, Haley thought, remembering the ambitious plans he'd recited to her only a few minutes before. *It must mean something that I keep thinking about Devon and Alex, even when I'm with Reese. Maybe I should keep my options open instead of mooning over a guy who's impossible to pin down.* He'd certainly had enough chances to catch her in the past.

Then Reese served her a bowl of pumpkin pudding with a huge dollop of vanilla ice cream, and of course she felt the irresistible tug of his charm all over again.

● ● ●

Thanksgiving's here, and Haley has plenty to be thankful for. She can be thankful that Mitchell knows how to put together what he takes apart. That Joan is not such an antisugar fascist that she'd embarrass Haley in front of the Highlands and refuse to allow their delicious desserts into the house. Most of all, Haley is thankful to the kitchen gods for breaking the Highlands' oven at this very opportune moment and letting her spend a long day of feasting her eyes on the delectable Reese.

But when the weekend is over, then what? Back to the grind of school and Reese's endless list of activities to keep them apart. And back to the temptations of Alex, Devon and who knows who else? It's all a bit much.

Still, Reese is right about one thing: with her academic schedule pretty much under control, Haley could use a new activity to beef up her transcript. The question is, what should it be? Should Haley try to tag along with Reese, in hopes of spending more time with him and cementing their relationship? Or is that a lost cause? Should she strike out on her own, indulge her independent streak and find a cause of her own to champion? Maybe she should surrender to genetics and admit that she's an environmentalist at heart.

If you want Haley to follow in her parents' footsteps

and join Annie Armstrong's pro-environment group, Planet Please, turn to page 21 (PLANETARY PROBLE-MAS). If you think Haley shouldn't give up on Reese so easily, have her stick closer to him by going to page 31 (BOYS DO CRY).

Will Haley still be thankful by Christmas? Or will she find cause for regret? Her fate is in your hands.

PLANETARY PROBLEMAS

No one likes a prophet
of doom.

TO: All 11th-grade girls at
    Hillsdale High
FROM: Her Divinity, Coco De Clerq
    (all hail!)
RE: Pushy little upstarts

Girls,
   It has come to my attention
that Annie Armstrong, about as
nobody a nobody as anyone can be

in the hierarchy of Hillsdale, has
started at least four new clubs
this semester and may have plans
for more. I don't know exactly
what she's up to, but I smell a
lame attempt to take over the
school. (And when I say smell,
I mean literally smell—as anyone
who's been within sniffing
distance of her manic nutjob
boyfriend, Dave Metzger, can
attest.) As I'm sure you all
understand, school takeover cannot
be tolerated in any way, shape or
form. I don't know who Annie
thinks she is, but I can tell you
what she totally, totally isn't,
and that's a class leader.

That, darlings, is why you will
all avoid little Miss Armstrong's
many "projects" like the West Nile
virus. If you know what's good for
you, that is. And I think you do.
Remember, I've got the power of
the whole state of New Jersey
behind me now, so I'm not fooling
around. This isn't kid stuff,
people. I shall be obeyed!

Coco

"Didn't you get the memo?" Coco De Clerq stopped Haley as she crossed the rotunda after school on her way to the first meeting of Annie Armstrong's new save-the-environment club, Planet Please. "No Annie Armstrong activities allowed."

The usual suspects draped themselves around the stone tables in the exclusive upperclassman hangout: skinny, overdone Coco in her expensive designer dress and boots; blond, voluptuous Whitney Klein wearing her own designs and trading jokes with her new stepsister-to-be, lanky soccer goddess Sasha Lewis, and Sasha's rocker boyfriend, Johnny Lane; and dark, funky cheerleader Cecily Watson in the lap of her boyfriend, football player Drew Napolitano. Hunky Spanish exchange student Sebastian Bodega leaned against a wall sipping coffee with his compatriot, the leggy model Mia Delgado. Laughing in a far corner were arty eccentrics Irene Chen and her boyfriend, Shaun Willkommen. And jumping over the stairs on their beat-up skateboards were Garrett "the Troll" Noll and a thug known only as Chopper.

"I got the memo," Haley said. "And I decided to ignore it."

Haley had spotted Coco arriving at school that morning in an entourage of gas-guzzling SUVs, wearing a fur-trimmed jacket, and that had sealed the deal. If the Cocos of the world were wasting its natural resources with such reckless abandon, somebody had to do something to offset the damage, and fast.

"Big mistake, Miller," Coco warned. "I don't send out memos only to have them ignored. You just ruined your junior year."

"Whatever." Coco's warnings used to intimidate Haley, but since Coco had experienced a few humiliations of her own, they'd lost a bit of their sting. Haley walked away.

"Saving the environment is such a giant cliché!" Coco called after her. "Annie Armstrong is social bird flu, don't you know that? Okay then, have fun with the dorks!"

Haley knew that associating with uptight Annie wasn't the coolest thing to do, socially speaking, but she had decided she didn't care. Some things were bigger than popularity; some things were more important. Haley had resolved that it was far better to stand up for what she believed in than to be intimidated by peer pressure. And she believed in a green planet.

Just ahead, outside the debate room, which doubled as Planet Please's new headquarters, Haley noticed more commotion. A guy was picketing in front of the classroom with a homemade sign. He was alone but was making a lot of noise.

"Stop the madness!" he shouted. "Global warming is a myth! You want to see a waste of resources? *This* is a waste of resources! *School* resources! Environmental activists are wasting time, money, paper— everything—on a false premise!"

Haley's heart sank. The protester was none other than Alex Martin, preppy senior and cocaptain of the debate team. Haley had always thought he was kind of cute for a conservative. Heck, he was cute regardless of his political ideology. But cuteness didn't excuse this.

Alex marched up and down in front of the debate room, with its PLEASE JOIN PLANET PLEASE NOW! sign taped on the door, in his khakis and blue button-down shirt, his side-parted chestnut hair sticking up slightly in the back. He waved his sign, which said GLOBAL WARMING IS A MYTH on one side and FACE THE TRUTH! BOYCOTT PLANET PLEASE! on the other.

Haley tried to sneak past Alex, but there was no getting past him. "Haley! Where do you think you're going?"

"To a meeting," Haley said. "I'm all for free speech, but you're way off base on this." She reached for the doorknob.

"Don't go in there!" Alex shouted. "Global warming is a lie. You're all being brainwashed! If anything, we're heading into another ice age. Face the truth! And don't waste your time on a nonexistent problem. Come on, Haley—a smart girl like you could be such an asset for the conservative cause."

"Sorry, Alex, but that's just not my thing," Haley said.

The door opened and Annie popped her head out. "Oh good! Another recruit. Get in here, Haley. Just ignore that maniac."

Haley went inside and shut the door on Alex's shouts of "I speak the truth! You can't ignore it forever!"

What a shame, Haley thought. How could such a bright guy be so clueless at the same time? It was a mystery. Still, she couldn't help admiring his courage and persistence; it took guts to stand up in the face of such overwhelming scientific evidence.

She surveyed the room and was disappointed to see that Coco's memo had done its work. Planet Please had drawn only four other members: Dave Metzger, who had to be there because Annie was his girlfriend; Ryan McNally, a recycling fanatic known as "the cleanup kid"; Dale Smithwick, one of Annie's debate team cronies; and Hannah Moss, a tiny genius who had skipped several grades and was both a friend and competitor to Annie and Dave. Haley settled into a seat by the window overlooking the school parking lot.

"Looks like this is about as many people as we can expect, with Alex out there scaring everybody away and Coco blackballing anyone who joins the club," Annie said. "So let's get started. The mission of Planet Please, as you know, could not be simpler: to bring awareness of the dangers of global warming to Hillsdale, to activate the student body to reduce wasteful consumption, and to force Washington to face the issue and do something about it. The question is, where to start? I have a few ideas, but I'd like to hear from you guys. Hannah?"

"I say our first goal should be greening up the cafeteria," Hannah said. "They could do a lot more to recycle drink cartons, they could stop using those chemical foam cups for drinks. . . ."

As the group batted ideas around, Haley found her attention drifting out the window to the gray weather. The parking lot was still nearly full of cars, since most kids had after-school activities until dinnertime. But the familiar roar of a rusty engine rattled from a far corner of the lot. Haley saw exhaust pouring from the back of a beat-up old convertible, the top down in spite of the threat of rain. She recognized the car instantly—it belonged to Devon McKnight, who sat in the driver's seat, his messy light brown hair blowing in the stormy breeze. But who was that beside him? The girl was facing Devon, so Haley couldn't quite tell who she was; she could only make out the neon blond hair. Devon gunned the engine and the car roared out of the lot with a squeal of tires, leaving the mystery of the blonde's identity unsolved.

During lulls in the meeting, Haley found herself thinking about Devon. Haley was surprised at how chilly she felt toward the girl in the passenger seat, whoever she was. Why? She knew it wasn't quite fair, given that she hadn't so much as spoken to

Devon in a couple of weeks. He couldn't be expected to maintain his unrequited crush on her forever. But what if he didn't have feelings for Haley anymore? What if he'd moved on and found someone new to like? Someone who liked him back? How would Haley feel about that?

Fine, she told herself. *I'd feel just fine. We come from different worlds. It would never have worked.* But the idea of Devon with a girlfriend still rankled.

Then something happened that made her forget all about the blonde. Mrs. Highland's car sped into the lot—she was driving uncharacteristically fast— and stopped at the end closest to the athletic fields. Reese hobbled toward the car—on crutches! Mrs. Highland got out and opened the passenger door for her son. One of Reese's soccer teammates helped him in and shut the door behind him. The car sped away, presumably to some medical office or emergency room.

"Haley, are you with us?" Annie asked.

"Huh?" Haley looked away from the window, feeling a tad panicky. What had happened to Reese? Suddenly, his welfare seemed more important—in the short run, anyway—than the destruction of the planet.

At that moment, the door flew open and Alex leaned into the room. "How's it going in here, kids? Save the planet yet?"

"Get out of here, Alex," Annie snapped.

"Gladly," Alex said. "I hate the smell of chlorophyll in the afternoon. But before I go, I'd like to announce that I am forming an environmental club of my own. It's called the Global Warming Is a Myth club, or GWIM, if you will. You're all welcome to join once you wake up and realize this country was founded on business principles, not charity for plants and birds. Cheers! And may the better environmental club win."

● ● ●

Haley's being torn in several conflicting directions. Unfortunately, she can't do everything at once. But which way should she go?

Alex is certainly stirring up trouble. His anti-environment club has Haley fuming, and one can't help wondering if that's the point. Does he really believe all this stuff he's spouting? What if it's just a ruse to rile Haley up and draw her closer to him? Boys do funny things when they want to get a girl's attention. Maybe all Alex needs is someone to lead him to the truth. Someone like, say, Haley Miller? What's the harm in hearing him out?

If you think Haley should give Alex a chance—and take a chance on reforming him—send her to page 46 (EYE-OPENER). On the other hand, what if Alex is serious? If you think he must be stopped at all costs and

Haley's the one to do it, have her get behind Annie Armstrong and defend a good cause on page 41 (BULLY-HORN).

Maybe Haley's more curious about who's cruising around in Devon's car. If that's what you believe, go on to page 58 (BLOND AMBITION). Finally, to have Haley go check up on Reese and find out what happened on the soccer field, turn to page 69 (OUT OF COMMISSION).

Three different boys, three very different problems. Should Haley defend her principles, satisfy her curiosity or show concern for her neighbor's welfare? The answer is in your page-turning little hands.

Mud is for slipping and mud is for slinging. Either way, mud is not your friend.

"Last soccer game of the season," Haley said as she huddled on the bleachers with Whitney Klein and Sasha Lewis. She'd come to support Reese and the rest of the Hillsdale varsity squad against rival Old Tappan.

Whitney adjusted her clear plastic raincoat and glanced at the sky. "I heard it's going to rain. I swear if it starts I'm out of here."

"Toughen up, Whit," Sasha said. "How can you possibly get wet? You're totally encased in plastic."

"Still, I don't care if it is the last soccer game of the season, I don't do rain."

Haley and Sasha exchanged an affectionate eye roll behind Whitney's back. When Haley had first arrived at Hillsdale, Whitney and Sasha had been part of a school-ruling—make that school-terrorizing—brat pack led by queen bee Coco De Clerq. A lot had happened since those bad old days. When his mother had won the gubernatorial election a few weeks earlier, Coco's boyfriend, Spencer Eton, had become the First Son of the State of New Jersey, and Coco was now too busy being First Girlfriend to bother with commoners like her old friends. The trio had already drifted apart anyway. Now Whitney's mom was living with Sasha's dad, so Whitney and Sasha had become unlikely sort-of stepsisters. Sasha was tall, athletic and musical, with long blond hair—a natural golden girl. Whitney was also blond but curvier and ditzier. Their family dramas had brought them close again, in spite of their personality differences. They spent their weekends wearing clothes Whitney designed for her fashion line, WK, and cruising in Sasha's '69 Mustang, Stallion.

"Go, Reese!" Haley shouted. The score was tied 1–1, and Old Tappan had the ball. But Reese Highland intercepted it and started dribbling down the field. He passed to Zach Woolsey, who took a shot at the goal and missed.

"No!" Sasha yelled. "Not to Zach! Don't pass to Zach!"

"What just happened?" Whitney asked. She liked going to games but rarely paid attention to the action on the field. The action in the bleachers was more her speed. Sebastian Bodega and Mia Delgado, two gorgeous Spanish exchange students, had just sat down to watch the game for a few minutes. They had a strange, ambiguous relationship—Sebastian called Mia his ex-girlfriend, but Haley thought he still seemed hung up on her.

"Zach's been weak lately," Sasha explained. "His head's not in it or something."

It began to drizzle. "Look, it's raining!" Whitney whined. "Can we get out of here, please?"

"There's only two minutes left on the clock," Haley said. "The game will be over soon."

"You can wait two minutes, can't you, Whit?" Sasha said.

"But the game's tied," Whitney said. "What if they go into overtime?"

"They won't," Haley said. "Reese is going to score any second now. Look—there he goes!"

Zach had the ball again. Reese sprinted down the field toward the goal, trying to dodge Old Tappan's defenders so that he could get open for a pass. He darted left and right, but the field was slippery. An Old Tappan player blocked him and Reese fell face-first in the mud.

"Foul! Illegal pushing!" Haley shouted, but the ref didn't call it.

"That was totally illegal," Sasha said. "They can't let them get away with that!"

Whitney opened her clear pink bubble umbrella. "Can we go now?"

Haley and Sasha ignored her. Reese got to his feet and wiped the mud from his face. He favored his right leg but shook off any help.

"He's limping," Haley said. "It looks like he hurt his left ankle."

The coach ran onto the field to talk to Reese, but Reese kept shaking his head as if to say "I'm all right, I'm fine." He stayed in the game. The ref blew the whistle and play resumed. Reese jogged down the field, but not at his usual speed.

"He shouldn't be playing on that ankle," Sasha said. "Look at him—he's not himself. He can barely run."

Haley watched Reese with concern. It was so typical of him to power through a game this way, to try to be a hero. She admired this quality in him and found it annoying at the same time. Of course it was admirable to put the team first, above your own health. But sometimes, Haley thought, it was a kind of vanity. In the end, self-sacrifice didn't always help the team. It only helped the self-sacrificer feel good about himself.

Someone passed the ball to Reese, and he dribbled down the field. But in his injured state, an Old Tappan player was able to swipe the ball from him easily. The Hillsdale crowd screamed as the Old Tappan forward drilled toward the goal. Haley glanced at the clock—ten seconds left.

"No! No! No!" Sasha yelled. "Get it! Get it! Get it!"

The Old Tappan player smacked the ball at Hillsdale's goalie. It whizzed past the goalie's fingertips into the goal. The buzzer sounded the end of the game. A collective groan rose from the soggy crowd.

Old Tappan won, 2–1.

"That sucks," Whitney said. "Now can we go? My hair is frizzing beyond belief."

"Sure, we can go now," Sasha said.

The Old Tappan boys yelped and jumped all over each other like puppies, while the Hillsdale boys hung their heads and filed off the field. "Good season, guys," Haley called to them, even though she knew it was useless to try to cheer them up. Reese looked up and threw her a weak smile. He was limping more dramatically now, and Zach was blinking away tears of disappointment.

"I guess boys do cry." Haley turned to see Coco stepping out of a sleek black SUV and sneering at the losing team. A beefy man in a dark suit protected her from the rain with a large navy umbrella. Spencer followed her out of the car, flanked by two more goons.

"Three security guards plus a driver for just the two of them," Haley muttered. "Mrs. Eton certainly wants to keep an eye on her son."

Sasha and Whitney snickered in agreement. Spencer Eton was well known about Hillsdale as something of a ne'er-do-well. To put it mildly.

Coco linked arms with Spencer as she mocked the losing team. "I guess it's a good thing we missed the game. Doesn't look like things turned out too well."

"I told you, soccer's a bore," Spencer said. "Unless you've got money riding on the outcome. And I knew better than to bet on these losers. The girls are another story."

He grinned at Haley, Sasha and Whitney, who were descending the bleachers and heading for Sasha's car. Coco stifled a gasp, shocked and annoyed to see the three of them—especially her old shadow, Whitney, and her old sidekick, Sasha—together without her. It just wasn't right.

"Hello, Haley," Coco said, blatantly ignoring her two former best friends. "You're slumming again, I see."

"You too," Haley said.

"Ha-ha." Clearly Coco thought it was impossible to be slumming in a chauffeured black SUV, attended by bodyguards, no matter who you were with. "What are you doing now, Haley?"

"The usual," Haley replied. Which actually meant going home and doing homework.

"We're headed over to the governor's mansion," Coco said. "Mrs. Eton wants my opinion on renovations—everything has to be perfect for the inauguration in January, you know. Haley, you should totally come over for a tour sometime—shouldn't she, Spence? It's so gorgeous, it makes the country club look like a bus depot. And I can tell you the whole history of the house and point out all the architectural details. You won't believe the lintels and the balustrades."

"The what?" Haley said. She had no idea what Coco was talking about—and she had a feeling Coco didn't entirely either.

Coco pretended to laugh. "You're so funny, Haley. Anyway, you should come over to my place this weekend. My parents are out of town."

Haley had to admit that the warm, dry SUV looked inviting, and it would be fun to see the governor's mansion at some point. Friendship with Coco always had its perks. There was a reason she was feared and revered at Hillsdale High. Coco had a certain magnetic power that sucked you in and, as soon as she was ready, spit you back out.

Haley wasn't sure if hanging out at Coco's house this weekend was the best idea, even with her parents out of town. But before she could give an answer, her attention was drawn to the roar of a rusty old engine. Across the parking lot, she spotted Devon McKnight's beat-up convertible—top down, in spite of the rain. He took a speed bump at thirty miles an hour and caught air. Someone with extremely blond hair sat beside him in the passenger seat. Haley could tell it was a girl, but from that distance, she couldn't make out who it was.

"Ugh, that's so *Dukes of Hazzard* trashy," Coco sniffed.

"Devon should drive more carefully," Whitney said. "Especially when it's raining."

"Maybe he's driving that way *because* it's raining," Haley suggested. "I think that convertible top doesn't always work."

"And how would *you* know *that*?" Coco demanded.

Luckily, Sasha changed the subject. "Who was that girl with him?" she asked.

Haley wondered the same thing. She had thought—and kind of hoped—that Devon still had his long-standing crush on her. But maybe she was wrong. Maybe he was on to the next thing.

The rain came down harder. Whitney stamped her foot. "I'm getting out of this muck. Let's go, Sasha. You coming, Haley?"

"Um, sure," Haley said.

"So, see you this weekend, Haley?" Coco asked.

● ● ●

Coco's got nerve, singling out Haley this way and ignoring her former BFFs. But sometimes Haley likes being singled out. Does she want to find out what Coco and Spencer will get up to this weekend while the De Clerq parents are out of town? While parents are away, the kids will play. . . .

But what about Reese? A sprained ankle usually isn't serious—but is that all this was? Just how hurt is he? And does he need Haley's help and tender loving care? Or at least her support? If she doesn't go to the locker room to check on him, what will he think? That she doesn't care? On the other hand, if she does go, maybe he'll put on his brave-soldier act and pretend nothing's wrong. It might be the nicest thing she could do for him—or it might lead nowhere. With Reese, you never know.

And who's Devon's mystery chick? Inquiring minds want to know—but does Haley? He sure seemed to be into Haley, in his own shy, commitment-averse way. But maybe he's just not that into her anymore. Or it could be nothing. The blonde he was speeding away with could be just a friend, right? Right?! If Haley lets Devon slip through her fingers now, she may never get him back.

So what should Haley do with the rest of this rainy day? Should she follow Coco's (mis)lead and mingle with the rich and powerful? If you think she shouldn't pass up this chance to see her government at work (and play), go to page 74 (RIVALRIES RESUMED).

Maybe you think Coco's getting way too wrapped up in being First Girlfriend, and Haley should avoid getting pulled into her sticky web of schemes. Sasha and Whitney are nicer people, right? If you think Haley should stick with them, turn to page 83 (SISTERLY LOVE).

Or perhaps Haley shouldn't focus on the girls so much—what about the boys? The girls can wait for a little while. Besides, Reese is hurt! What kind of neighbor—or more—would Haley be if she didn't make sure he was all right? If you think the right thing to do is check on Reese and his sore ankle, turn to OUT OF COMMISSION on page 69.

And then there's Devon. If you think Haley has got to know who the blonde riding shotgun with him was—and she's got to know *now*—send her to page 58 (BLOND AMBITION).

Haley's a lucky girl. She's got lots of opportunities at her fingertips. The trouble is, choosing one eliminates the others—no girl gets to have everything.

A bullhorn isn't always the best way to get a message across.

"What's taking him so long?" Annie asked.

She and Haley were waiting in the school parking lot for Alex Martin to emerge from the building. Armed with bullhorns and signs, they planned to stop his heinous Global Warming Is a Myth club before it could start. Students milled about in the parking lot and the courtyard and flowed out of the school in a steady stream, providing a good audience.

"He's probably having an after-school snack,"

Haley said. "Endangered hawk eggs washed down with panda blood."

"Someone's coming." Annie grabbed Haley's arm. "Bullhorns in hectoring position!"

Haley poised hers near her mouth as Alex walked out of the school building, backpack over his shoulder, wiping something red from his mouth. It was probably just cranberry juice, but to Haley it might as well have been panda blood. Or something worse.

"It's him!" Annie cried. "Go!"

"Stop GWIM!" Haley and Annie shouted through their megaphones. "Global warming is not a myth!"

"Global warming is a fact!" Haley cried. "Fact: The polar ice caps are melting at an unprecedented rate! Fact: The sea level is rising! Fact: Residents of more than one Pacific island have already been forced to relocate due to rising sea levels! Fact . . ."

As Haley ranted, a small crowd gathered. Alex stood on the school steps, listening for a few seconds and grinning in an infuriatingly smug way. Then he disappeared inside the school building.

"Where did he go?" Annie asked. "Do you think he's given up already?"

"Probably," Haley said. "Wow, it's amazing how powerful one of those things can be." She lifted the megaphone to her lips and shouted to the crowd,

"Look—he's already beaten! Alex Martin's anti-environment club has no chance against the facts!"

"Not so fast." Alex reappeared on the steps, this time with a bullhorn of his own. An even bigger, more powerful bullhorn.

"He's armed!" Annie cried. "Where did he get that thing?"

"He was ready for us," Haley whispered, stunned.

"Shouting won't make GWIM go away!" Alex roared through his bullhorn. "I suggest you check your so-called facts. Just because someone posted something on a Web site for tree-hugging patsies doesn't make it true. Do your homework! This glacial melting has happened before—it's all part of the natural cycle of the planet. Human consumption and carbon emissions have nothing to do with it."

"You're the one reading lunatic Web sites," Haley shouted back. "Why don't *you* do *your* homework? The scientists of the world—respectable scientists, that is—are on my side, not yours!"

"You mean anti-American scientists," Alex said, and a few members of the crowd clapped. "Remember how cold it was last winter? What about the cool, rainy summer we just had? That doesn't feel like global warming to me!" More applause and cheering as the crowd drifted toward Alex and away from Haley. She had to get them back.

"This is a worldwide problem, not an American one," she said. "We're all affected. Now is the time to face the truth, stop wasting our resources and work together as a international coalition!"

"Yeah!" A few people in the crowd clapped for Haley. But Alex wasn't finished yet.

"Trying to fix global warming is impossible," Alex said. "And it will hurt our economy. Workers will lose their jobs. People like you and me will lose their houses. Think of it! Is it more important to save a bird species or a family? What if it was your family— which would you choose?"

"My family!" a boy shouted. "Global warming is a myth!"

Several other onlookers joined in the chant, and soon Alex was leading the crowd in a chorus of "Global warming is a myth! Global warming is a myth!"

"No it's not! No it's not!" Haley and Annie yelled, straining their voices to be heard over the crowd. The girls had their supporters, but a lot of people had drifted over to Alex's cause and were laughing and chanting along with him.

"Don't let these doomsayers tell us what to do!" Alex called out. "Join my club! Join GWIM! Together we can drown out the negative Nellies who just want to keep us from living the good life!"

"Hurray!" most of the kids shouted.

"Boo!" shouted Haley and Annie and their few straggling supporters.

• • •

What happened? Haley's pro-environment demonstration devolved into a shouting match. Not only did their point get lost in the uproar, but they also lost supporters to Alex's group. And any chance of open discussion—which could have more effectively changed people's minds—has been demolished. GWIM has more supporters than ever. The biggest loser here: the environment, Annie's Planet Please club and Haley. Next time, she should try a little finesse if she wants to sway the hearts and minds of her schoolmates. If there is a next time.

Go back to page 1.

You can catch more flies with honey than you can with, um . . . bullhorns.

"The problem with all you jolly green jokers is you claim to be open-minded, but you're actually unwilling to listen to any argument that doesn't fit your agenda," Alex Martin said. "You're all totally close-minded."

"That's not true," Haley said. "I'll prove it to you. I want to hear your side—really."

After the first Planet Please meeting, Haley left the headquarters to find Alex still pacing the hall with his GLOBAL WARMING IS A MYTH! sign. Annie

Armstrong had looked stunned when Haley stopped to talk to him.

"He's all yours," Annie said with a shrug as she and the others left.

But Haley had a secret plan: she was going to change Alex's mind about the state of the planet. She was sure she could do it; he was intelligent, after all, and in spite of his inflammatory rhetoric, she sensed that a thoughtful, sensitive soul was longing to breathe free beneath the conservative bluster. At least, she hoped so. *No one that cute should be so . . . wrong,* Haley thought.

"What are you doing now?" she asked him.

"Now?" Alex let his sign fall. There was no one left to protest to. The school was emptying, and he and Haley were two of the last people left in the hall. "You mean, now?"

"Right now," Haley said. "Would you like to come over to my house? We could have a little snack and you could explain to me why global warming is a myth. It's quiet there; we'll be able to talk."

"Well . . . sure." Haley had caught him off guard. All part of her plan. "Why not?"

"Excellent. Let's go." Haley's dad wasn't teaching that afternoon and was sure to be home working on his new film. Haley would play devil's advocate, listening to Alex's arguments while her father presented the heart-wrenching evidence of environmental devastation he'd captured on film. Surely, she thought, Alex hadn't thought the whole thing through. There were aspects to global warming he wasn't aware of. Perry Miller was the perfect person to help Haley open Alex's eyes. And once open, maybe Alex would relax a little, soften and become someone Haley could get to know a little better. She certainly wanted to.

In the parking lot, Alex opened the passenger door of his preppy-looking but not very efficient wagon for Haley and helped her in. Kind of old-fashioned, but Haley couldn't help being charmed. They drove to the Miller homestead near Hillsdale Heights. She led him inside, and upstairs, where sure enough, her father was in his study.

"Hi, Dad," Haley said. "This is Alex."

Perry looked up from his work. "Nice to meet you, Alex. How was school today? Did they try to teach you anything about creationism? I have my doubts about that biology teacher. You two want something to eat? There's leftover bulgur salad in the fridge."

"Thanks," Haley said. "Where's Mitchell?" She didn't want him around to distract her from her mission. All she needed was for annoying little brother to start taking apart Alex's cell phone or something and the subject would effectively be changed for good.

"In his room," Perry said. "Building a space station out of spare radio parts, last I checked."

That should keep him busy for a while, Haley thought, leading Alex downstairs and into the kitchen. She offered him some sparkling water. He turned down the bulgur salad. "I totally understand," Haley said. "I wish I could offer you cookies or something in the way of a normal after-school snack, but this is a No Refined Sugar zone."

Alex nodded. "Makes sense. Now I see where you get your left-leaning tendencies."

"Well, that's exactly what I don't want," Haley confessed. "I mean, I know I'm influenced by my parents, but I'd like to hear the other side too. I'd like to think I can make up my own mind."

"That's very refreshing," Alex said. "You have no idea how rare that kind of thinking is these days."

Haley smiled and squeezed lime into his fizzy water.

Alex began to tell her about the evidence contradicting global warming—the places that had gotten cooler rather than warmer, the cycles of warming and cooling that the earth had undergone over the eons, the signs that erratic weather patterns predicted not warming but a coming ice age. Haley listened intently and nodded. "Very interesting," she said.

Then he talked about American coal, oil and lumber interests, how U.S. power depended on the strength of its industries and how the current high standard of living so many Americans enjoyed was at risk if the United States cut down on production or demand. "Even your own family drives an SUV," he said, nodding toward the driveway.

"It's a hybrid," Haley pointed out.

"Still," Alex said. "Look at this house. Do you really want to live without a dishwasher, a washer/dryer, air-conditioning and heat? Would you want to live in a smaller house and share a room with your brother?"

"Ha!" Haley scoffed. "Now that would be a nightmare. But I don't really see what that has to do with climate change."

"It has to do with the economy," Alex said. "With our resources and our wealth, and how they're distributed. It's all connected. The climate isn't just about climate. It's about everything."

"I totally agree," Haley said. "On the other hand, would I want to live in a big comfortable house while outside the air is unbreathable and the plants and animals are dying?"

"But there's no reason to believe that would happen," Alex said. "People are just trying to scare you. There's no factual basis for global warming—that's what I've been trying to tell you."

"Oh," Haley said. "I get it." She got it, all right. Alex was living in a conservative dream bubble, a bubble that needed to be popped.

With perfect timing, Perry walked into the

kitchen in search of a cup of tea. "Hey, kids," he said. "How's that bulgur salad?"

"Dad," Haley asked, "how's your new film?" She turned to Alex. "He's a documentary filmmaker."

"Oh, it's coming along," Perry said, suddenly sensing a receptive audience. "Would you like to see what I've got so far?"

This was exactly what Haley had hoped would happen. "Sure, I'd love to," she said innocently. "Alex?"

"Of course." Alex rose to his feet, ready to go into the den. Haley had counted on his polite interest in her father's work. Though he could well be genuinely interested, Haley thought.

Perry led them into the study. "The footage is very rough, so I apologize," he said. "I'm looking at the effects of climate change on migratory birds. Birds all over the world have been confused by the speedy rise in temperatures, and their migrations reflect that. Some of them don't bother to migrate at all anymore, because their nesting habitats have gotten so warm they don't need to fly south for winter."

"Doesn't sound so bad to me," Alex said. "I hate commuting."

"Well," Perry said, "they end up fighting for scarce resources, not having enough food to eat, falling victim to predators. And their schedules don't sync with plant growth anymore, so pollination doesn't occur, and then the plants stop growing. . . . The problem is spreading throughout the ecosystem. Watch."

He started showing some of his footage. Alex sat back with his arms crossed over his chest, as if nothing Perry showed him could change his mind.

The film began with a small, beautiful songbird, with a yellow head and belly, looking for a place to land on a coastline filled with highways and beach development. "This used to be marshland, a resting stop for these birds on their way from New England to the West Indies," Perry said. "But development has left them no safe place to stop." One of the birds dropped into the ocean, looking exhausted. A larger, predatory seabird swooped down to snatch it up. "Their numbers are diminishing fast."

"What kind of bird is it?" Alex asked.

"The Cape May warbler." The film showed the bird in a spruce tree, chirping.

"Cape May?" Alex said. "My family has a house in Cape May. I've heard that chirp when we're down there on fall weekends."

Aha, Haley thought. *Got him.*

Perry talked over the raw footage of the beautiful little bird struggling for survival. Global warming was predicted to drive up to thirty percent of all animal species to extinction by the year 2100, he explained. And the change in bird migration patterns—which meant that birds arrived at their destinations weeks earlier than in previous years—was just an early warning sign, incontrovertible proof that the climate was warming up. Alex watched the bird, so familiar from his childhood beach vacations, with growing alarm on his face.

"As you said yourself, it's all connected," Haley said. "The birds to the plants and insects, to the food supply, to human life on earth. How can there be any economy if there's no food to support the population? Who needs a job when there's nothing to eat?"

"I have to admit, this is disturbing," Alex said. Haley had to stop herself from smiling in triumph. Disturbing! His face had turned white.

The front door opened and Joan Miller stumbled in with armloads of groceries. "Anybody home?"

Perry hurried over to help her with the bags, as Alex jumped up and offered to assist too. "Thanks, both of you," Joan said, casting an approving glance in Haley's direction.

"Mom, this is Alex Martin," Haley said.

"Nice to meet you, Mrs. Miller," Alex said. "We were just admiring your husband's work-in-progress."

"Were you?" Joan headed into the kitchen, and the others followed with the grocery bags. "Alex Martin? I know that name. Aren't you captain of the debate team? With Annie Armstrong?"

"Guilty as charged." Alex set the bags on the counter and leaned against it, his confidence returning.

"That's funny," Joan said. "I work with Annie's mother, Blythe." She paused, glancing from Alex to Haley as if she wasn't sure whether she should continue.

"What is it?" Haley asked.

"Well, I suppose you'll hear about it from Annie eventually," Joan continued. "It seems that Nora Metzger has moved in with your art teacher—Mr. Von, is it?"

"Mrs. Metzger and Mr. Von?" Haley tried to take in this news. Nora Metzger was Dave Metzger's mother. Dave Metzger was Annie Armstrong's boyfriend. Mrs. Metzger was pretty much the most neurotic and uptight person Haley had ever met. She saw danger everywhere and had Dave convinced he was allergic to just about everything under the sun. She would have kept him in a bubble if she could. She was the last person Haley would imagine getting serious with anyone, much less the eccentric loosey goosey Rick Von, with his rumpled clothes, stubbly beard, whispery rasp of a voice and oddly lopsided walk.

On the other hand, maybe they made a weird kind of sense as a couple. They were both oddballs; at least they had that in common.

"So wait," Alex said. "You're saying they moved in together? So that means Dave Metzger is . . . living in Mr. Von's house now?"

Joan nodded. "Blythe told me that Annie's been over to visit several times."

"I can't believe Annie hasn't told us about this yet," Haley said.

"You know Annie and her obessions," Alex said. "Right now she's so obsessed with saving the planet that she sometimes forgets to go to the bathroom."

"Apparently the house is very rustic," Joan said. "Full of fascinating antiques and relics from the sixties."

Haley tried to imagine the household: Dave Metzger, nervous, sweaty, breaking out in hives at even the thought of strawberries, blueberries, apples, shellfish, regular fish, milk, all dairy products—in fact, pretty much anything but rice cakes—holed up in his new bedroom in Mr. Von's cobweb-filled house, taping his podcast, "Inside Hillsdale," and spouting his bizarre conspiracy theories while his mother and Mr. Von made out or whatever downstairs. How would Mr. Von treat Dave at school? Would he act all fatherly or pretend nothing had changed?

Haley looked at her own mother and shuddered. Thank God her parents were still married. There'd been plenty of strange parental pairings in Hillsdale over the past year or so, some of them not so bad, like Sasha Lewis's father and Whitney Klein's mother. But a few of them struck Haley as crimes against nature. She couldn't imagine having to move in with one of her teachers—especially Mr. Von.

"So what did you think of Perry's movie so far?" Joan asked Alex, mercifully changing the subject.

"Impressive," Alex said. "And a little scary. I have to admit he makes a good case."

Haley smiled at him. "So you're going to rethink your whole global-warming-is-a-myth stance? Maybe forget about the club? Maybe even join Planet Please?"

"I didn't say that," Alex said, grinning wryly.

● ● ●

Has Haley worked her magic on Alex and his anti-environmental views? Results inconclusive. But there are hopeful signs. It was good of her to try, anyway. But even the fate of the Cape May warbler is easily trumped by local gossip like Joan's—no wonder Haley and Alex were distracted.

Dave Metzger, Mrs. Metzger and Mr. Von together in the same house? It boggles the mind.

Haley has a good imagination, but even she can't quite picture it. To send her chez Von to see the weird menagerie for herself, go to page 89 (GARAGE BANDWIDTH). Dave is sure to be video-podcasting, and that's usually an event in itself.

So how are things going with Alex? Frankly, it's hard to tell. Do you think he's too conservative for Haley and that she'll never change him no matter how much film footage Perry shows him? Maybe she and Alex just don't have the right chemistry. But if they don't, whose molecules *do* have Haley's atomic number?

If you think Haley's still daydreaming about Devon McKnight go to page 96 (TAKE THE LEAD).

Maybe you think Haley should forget about Dave and Devon and leave her options open. Perhaps she should raid Joan's jewelry box and borrow something of sentimental value, just to see what kind of luck it attracts. If so, go to page 101 (FAMILY JEWELS).

Haley hasn't committed herself to any one path yet, so you still have time to steer her in the right direction— or the wrong one. Just watch your step, or she could end up in an unhappy place.

BLOND AMBITION

Haley's not
the only one with
an intriguing neighbor.

"Haley Daley Dumpling! Over here!"

As soon as Haley walked into the Golden Dynasty, Shaun Willkommen waved her over to his booth. The restaurant was quiet, since it was four o'clock, during the lull between lunch and dinner, and the only people in the place were Hillsdale High students stopping in for an afternoon pig-out. Haley followed Shaun's beckoning arm to the booth in the back corner, where she found him with his girlfriend, Irene Chen, and Devon McKnight. Irene's parents owned the restaurant, and Haley was surprised to see Irene sitting instead of working. Next to Devon was a skinny peroxide blonde Haley didn't know but had seen around—most recently riding shotgun in Devon's beat-up old convertible.

"Sit down." Shaun slid over to make room for Haley on his side of the booth. "The dim sum just arrived."

Haley grabbed a pair of chopsticks and dipped a veggie bun in soy sauce before Shaun could eat them all. With an outsized personality and a taste for all things weird—make that all things, period—Shaun was known for his huge appetite. However, his recent glories on the track and field team had shaved a few pounds off of his maximum weight.

"You know Darcy, right, Haley?" Irene nodded at the bottle blonde. "Darcy Podowski, Haley Miller."

"Hi," Darcy said.

"Hi," Haley said. "I've seen you around school."

"She's a freshman," Devon explained.

"And I live down the street from Devon," Darcy added.

"Right." Devon speared a dumpling and bit off the end. "So now that she goes to the high school we've got a park-and-ride thing going." He laughed, and Darcy tickled his rib with her chopsticks. "Hey," Devon said. "Don't get soy sauce on my shirt. This is a Jack's Vintage original." Devon worked at Jack's Vintage Clothing store part-time, allowing Shawn, Irene and Haley to get clothes for practically free.

"Like you care," Darcy said, tickling him again. Devon didn't seem to mind, it was true. He just laughed and tried to tickle her right back. They certainly were comfortable with each other—a little too comfortable, in Haley's opinion.

Park and ride? Haley thought. What did Devon mean by *park*? Or by *ride,* for that matter?

"I've got soy sauce stains on just about everything I own," Shaun said. "Since I met Rini here, I'm not one to worry about neatness."

"That's for sure," Irene said.

"I love my soy sauce stains," Shaun said. "They're my little love marks."

"Soon to be ex-girlfriend if you keep walking around looking like the victim of a food fight," Irene warned.

"Speaking of exes. . . ," Darcy said. "What's Rose up to these days?" Darcy stole a fried noodle from Devon's plate.

Devon shot Darcy a "shut up" look. Clearly this was not a topic of conversation he wanted introduced.

Hmm, Haley thought. *What's this all about?*

"Who's Rose?" Irene asked.

"Nobody." Devon sank a bit in his seat. He clearly wanted to avoid the subject.

"She's Devon's ex," Darcy explained. "From art school."

Devon had transferred to Hillsdale High from an art school in the city the previous year. In the time Haley had known him, he'd never once mentioned an ex-girlfriend, or anyone named Rose for that matter, to her. So how did this Darcy know so much about his personal life, if all Devon did was give her a ride to school?

Or *was* that all they did together?

"Dude, tell," Shaun said to Devon. "What's the story of Rose?"

"There's nothing to tell," Devon said, glaring again at Darcy, who looked pleased with herself. "I swear. Rose was a girl I knew in art school, end of story."

Haley had a feeling that wasn't the end of the story, but she decided not to press the issue—yet.

"Hot and sour soup?" A waiter appeared with a trayful of soup bowls and set them on the table.

"Take mine, Haley." Irene passed her bowl down the table. "I'm sick of this stuff."

"I'll never get sick of it." Shaun lifted his bowl and took a huge slurp of soup. "Ow! Hot! Mm, sour. Ow! Hot! Mm, sour."

Irene rolled her eyes. "You do that every time. I told you to let it cool first."

"Tsiser t'nac I doog os sllems ti tub, wonk I," Shaun said.

"What did he say?" Darcy asked. "Can he speak Chinese?"

" 'I know, but it smells so good,' " Irene translated. "Sometimes Shaun talks backwards. Just one of his many endearing quirks. Takes a little getting used to."

"Just like the rest of him," Haley teased.

"That's enough out of you, Red," Shaun said, tugging on a chunk of Haley's auburn hair.

"Shaun, no sticky fingers on other peoples' faces," Irene scolded.

"It's okay," Haley said. "I'm used to it. I've got a seven-year-old brother, remember?"

"Are my fingers chubby?" Shaun held up his thick, soft hand and stared at it in wonder. "I never thought of them that way."

"Oh, please," Irene said. "You're totally self-conscious about it. When he's alone in his room he secretly does this thing called hand aerobics in a vain attempt to make them thinner. It's the only part of his body that hasn't changed since he joined the track team."

"The *only* part?" Devon asked slyly, causing Darcy to erupt in a fit of giggles.

"Artists' hands should be slender," Shaun said. "Slender and expressive. Hand aerobics is a secret, Irene. You weren't supposed to tell."

"Sorry," Irene said. "I didn't know it was a *secret*

secret. I thought it was just one of those Shaun secrets, where you don't care who knows about it."

"What? Woman, from now on, assume everything I tell you is a secret secret unless otherwise informed."

"Sure. Whatever you say," Irene said.

"I've got skinny hands, Shaun, but it doesn't make me a good artist," Darcy said, lifting her left hand. On her wrist was a small, inky star.

"You are so a good artist," Devon said.

"I love your tat," Irene said, grabbing Darcy's hand to examine the tattoo.

"It's cool, isn't it?" Devon said. Haley bristled slightly.

"It's brutally awesome," Shaun said. "I've been wanting to get a tattoo forever, but I can't decide what to get. Like, as soon as I think for sure I want a mermaid, I change my mind and want a whale or something. There are too many choices out there."

"Why not get both?" Darcy said.

"She's right," Irene said. "You've got plenty of skin to cover."

Shaun grinned and slapped his rounded belly. Then he grabbed another dumpling. "The more of these I eat, the more skin I'll have to tattoo."

"That's one way to look at it," Devon said.

"I told Dev he should get a tat of a coat of arms,"

Darcy said. "You know, make one up. To play off his last name, McKnight."

Dev? Haley had never heard anyone call Devon "Dev" before, and it annoyed her for some reason.

"You could put a camera on the coat of arms," Irene said.

"And maybe a skateboard, or a thrift shop porkpie hat . . ."

"Or just do a big knight, in armor, on horseback, right across your chest." Shaun mimed ripping open his shirt like Superman to show off the imaginary knight tattoo gleaming on his chest. "That would be major. Maybe I should write *Willkommen* on my forehead, so everybody who sees me will feel Germanically welcome."

"What about you, Haley?" Devon asked. "What would you do if you got a tattoo?"

Haley wasn't at all certain she wanted to permanently mark up her skin. But everyone else at the table seemed to be so into the idea, so she thought she'd better say something.

"Maybe a tiny four-leaf clover," Haley said. "For luck. I like the star, too. But didn't it hurt, having a needle poking your wrist, Darcy?" Haley stroked her own wrist, trying to imagine it. "It's such a sensitive part of your body."

"Not as sensitive as some parts," Shaun said. Irene shot him a "shut up" look.

"It does hurt a little," Darcy said. "But not for long. And it's totally worth it."

The waiter reappeared to fill their water glasses and drop a small pile of fortune cookies on the table. Haley took one and broke it open.

"Read your fortune out loud," Irene said.

" 'A figure from your past will soon reappear,' " Haley read.

"Like a banana," Shaun said.

"What?" Haley said.

"You're supposed to add 'like a banana' at the end of your fortune, to make it more interesting," Shaun said.

"That's so stupid," Irene said. She opened her cookie and read her fortune. " 'You have many talents.' "

"Like a banana," Shaun said.

Irene smirked at him. "Read yours, Devon."

" 'You will soon find happiness,' " Devon read.

"Like a banana," Shaun added. "That's way profound." Haley thought she saw Devon blush. He looked down at the table so that he wouldn't have to catch anyone's eye. Darcy was staring right at him. She cracked open her cookie and read her fortune.

" 'Try to tame your restlessness,' " she read. "Like a banana."

"That doesn't really make sense," Haley said.

"Sure it does," Shaun said. "Bananas always

makes sense." He broke open another cookie. " 'You will have a comfortable old age' like a banana! See!"

"But bananas get brown and gooey after, like, a week," Irene protested.

"Speaking of old age," Shaun said. "Did you cats and kitties hear the latest freaky world news? Mr. Von, Acid Rick himself, is cohabitating with Dave Metzger's mommy dearest!"

"Are you kidding?" Haley said. Mr. Von was their eccentric art teacher, known for his rumpled clothes, permastubble beard and odd, whispery speaking voice. Dave Metzger, Annie Armstrong's boyfriend, was a basket case of allergies and nerves, most of which he'd inherited from his neurotic mother.

"I'm so not kidding," Shaun said. "Did you catch the last episode of 'Inside Hillsdale'? You could see Mr. Von and Dave's mom in the background for a second—holding hands! That's, like, evidence!"

"Who's Dave Metzger?" Darcy asked.

"He's the kid who does that video podcast, 'Inside Hillsdale.' You know, the one ranting and raving about cafeteria portions and parking spaces."

"He's a geek," Irene added.

"So Dave is living in Von's house?" Devon asked.

"You heard it here first," Shaun said. He belched for emphasis.

"What a freak show that must be," Irene added.

"I can't imagine living with a teacher," Haley said. "Or one of my parents dating one. Especially Mr. Von."

"Dave has always been kind of batty," Devon mused. "This could push him over the edge."

"Kind of batty?" Shaun said, fluffing his blond mullet. "Next to him I'm the poster child for normal. Who knows, maybe he likes it at Von's. Seems like Madman Metzger's found the cuckoo's nest."

"Do you think it's really true?" Irene said. "Maybe this is just one of those crazy rumors."

"Babe, a story that weird has got to be true," Shaun said.

● ● ●

Haley's just gotten a lot of new information to take in. Let's start with this girl Darcy Podowski. Where did she materialize from? Just how long—and how well—has she known Devon? All that talk about parking, ex-girlfriends and what kind of tattoo he should get could make a girl wonder.

Haley's always had a thing with Devon, a kind of mutual flirtation, but maybe she's been taking his interest for granted too long. If you think she should make an effort to head off Darcy and spend more time alone with Devon, have her TAKE THE LEAD on page 96.

Maybe Devon's not the one Haley should worry about. Dave Metzger's gotten himself into an odd situation, and he's not the best person to handle a sudden, difficult change. If you think Haley's dying to know whether Dave is really living in Mr. Von's spooky cottage these days, have her check it out on page 89 (GARAGE BANDWIDTH).

Then there's all that talk of tattoos. The art crowd certainly seems fascinated by them, but is Haley? If you think she should focus on less permanent accessories, go to page 101 (FAMILY JEWELS).

Sure, Haley wants to make her mark on the world But will it be with a tattoo needle?

OUT OF COMMISSION

Sometimes accidents happen for a reason, and sometimes they just happen.

"Haley, come on in." Barbara Highland greeted Haley at the front door. "What have you got there?"

"It's a hot fudge sundae," Haley said. "I picked it up on my way home from school. I heard what happened to Reese and I thought it might cheer him up."

"How sweet of you," Barbara said. "We just got back from the hospital. The X-rays were not good— he broke his foot in two places."

"That's terrible," Haley said. "Is he in a lot of pain?"

"A little," Mrs. Highland said. "He tries to be

stoic, but I can tell he's kind of low. Why don't you take that sundae upstairs to his room? I'm sure he'll appreciate it."

It was early in the evening after the last boys' soccer game of the season. In a heartbreaking loss to Old Tappan, Reese had injured his foot. Haley came home right away to find out how he was doing.

Upstairs, she found Reese propped up in bed, his left foot in a cast and elevated on a stack of pillows. He was absorbed in a history book, highlighter in hand. She tapped on the door and he turned his head.

"Hey." He smiled and put down his book. "Come on in."

"I brought you a treat." Haley gave him the ice cream. "How are you feeling?"

Reese lifted the cast an inch off the pillows. "Not so hot. Basketball season's out of the question, looks like."

"What a shame," Haley said, but secretly she couldn't help feeling just a little relieved. If Reese wasn't playing basketball, that left him lots of spare time—to spend, she hoped, with her. After all, he lived right next door, and with his foot in a cast he couldn't get very far. He'd be her captive audience, her patient, her charge. She could stop by every day and check on him, and soon he'd depend on her to bring him things he couldn't get for himself. . . .

"What will the Hawks do without you?" Haley said.

"They'll be fine," Reese said modestly. He was one of the star players. "Johnny Lane can carry the whole team by himself, practically."

"That's not true," Haley said. "They need you. They'll be terrible without you." She watched for a second as he ate a spoonful of hot fudge. "So what are you going to do with your free time now that you can't shoot hoops?"

"Well, in a way it's a blessing in disguise," Reese said. "I mean, not playing ball gives me that much more time to study."

Haley suppressed a sigh of frustration. *Great.* Even with his foot in a cast, held hostage next door, Reese would be too busy to see her.

"I figure, basketball practice is two hours a day, three if you count locker-room time," Reese said. "So each weekday I'll spend that time on a different subject. Monday: AP Calculus. Tuesday: AP History. Wednesday: AP English. . . ."

"And do I get squeezed in on Thursday, at least?" Haley teased, hoping to change the subject.

He finished the ice cream sundae and set the bowl aside. "You'll get all the time you want, as long as you promise to feed me. Can we go out to eat?"

Haley laughed. "You just demolished an entire hot fudge sundae."

"I know, but I'm still starving." Reese tapped his left leg. "I never realized how much energy healing a broken bone takes. Come on, let's go to Hap's. Some greasy comfort food ought to cure what ails me."

Haley's cell beeped. She checked the screen. It was a text from Sasha, asking her to come meet the crew at Bubbies Bistro. Haley guessed the usual suspects would be there: Sasha; her boyfriend, Johnny Lane; Cecily Watson and her boyfriend, Drew Napolitano; and probably Sasha's new best friend, her soon-to-be-stepsister, Whitney Klein.

"What do you say?" Reese asked. Haley wasn't sure how to respond.

● ● ●

Poor Reese. Out for the season. He doesn't seem to be in too much pain, though, and he's taking the whole broken-foot thing pretty well. Already up for going out to dinner. If only he'd schedule Haley into one of those empty afternoon basketball slots, she'd be all set.

That's not to be. However, Haley has a few interesting choices here. She could go to Hap's Diner with Reese, where they could be alone and talk. It would be about as close to a real date as they've gotten lately. If you think Haley needs to treasure every second she can get with Reese, send her to page 106 (CASTAWAY).

On the other hand, even with a broken foot, Reese can't be bothered to pencil Haley into his precious college-bound schedule. So maybe Haley doesn't have time for him, either. She has a life of her own, after all. She has friends. Plus, Hap's is sort of a dive, and not only is Bubbies Bistro more upscale, they also have the best turkey panini in town. If you think Haley would much rather have a fun night out with Sasha's crew at Bubbies, turn to page 122 (MAMMA MIA).

If you think Haley is too annoyed to indulge His Majesty another second but isn't in the mood for a raucous night out with her friends either, send her to page 101 (FAMILY JEWELS) and take a time-out.

Haley's choice is in your hands.

RIVALRIES RESUMED

Beware the sister who goes after your mister.

Haley rang the doorbell—more like door chimes—at the De Clerq McMansion. The door was opened by Consuela, the De Clerqs' housekeeper.

"*Hola,* Miss 'Aley, come in."

"Thank you, Consuela," Haley said, following the housekeeper through the ornate foyer, under the crystal chandelier and into the media room, where Coco, Spencer and Coco's older sister, Ali, lounged on matching leather couches. Ali and Spencer were in the middle of a fierce game of poker.

"You want something to drink?" Consuela asked Haley.

"Um, iced tea would be nice, I guess," Haley said. She'd never get used to being waited on by household servants. It just felt too weird.

"Iced tea," Spencer mocked. "It's five-thirty— we're well into cocktail hour. Make that a Long Island iced tea, Consuela."

"No, really," Haley said. "Plain old iced tea is fine for now."

"Are you going to join the party, or are you going to be your usual prudish self?" Spencer slurred slightly on the word "prudish."

Ali had been staring intently at the playing cards in her hand, but now she glanced up. "Leave her alone, Spencer," she said. "And deal." She took a swig of pale brown liquid from her crystal cocktail glass. Whiskey, no doubt.

Coco sat off to the side, curled on the couch with a pint of chocolate fudge ice cream in one hand and a soup spoon in the other. *Uh-oh—trouble.* The razor-thin, always-dieting Coco De Clerq eating ice cream— real, honest-to-God, full-fat ice cream—was an extremely bad sign. Something was seriously wrong.

"Haley," Coco said without enthusiasm. "You came. Good." She stuffed a spoonful of ice cream into her mouth.

Haley sat down on Coco's sofa and watched Spencer deal another hand. "Thank God Mom and

Dad are in Palm Beach this weekend," Ali said, studying her new cards. "I don't think I could handle them breathing down our necks every second. After a few months in college you get used to doing things your own way, know what I mean?"

Ali De Clerq was a freshman at Yale, home for the Thanksgiving holiday—which would explain the unhappy expression on Coco's face. Coco and Ali were very competitive, and one thing they used to fight over all the time was Spencer. Ali and Spencer always claimed they were just very close friends, but Coco had never quite trusted her big sis. Even Haley had to admit that sometimes it seemed as though there was more going on between Ali and Spencer, no matter how heartily they protested their innocence.

"Totally," Spencer said. "I can't wait to get the hell out of here and be on my own. That's one thing I miss about boarding school."

Haley suppressed an incredulous laugh and glanced at Coco, who miserably sucked on her spoon. Coco had more freedom and less supervision than almost anybody at Hillsdale High except Spencer—at least, until his mother's recent election. The De Clerq *père* and *mère* were always partying or jetting off to some glamorous destination, and Spencer's mother was busy with her political career. No one could stop Spencer, who'd been kicked out of more than one boarding school, from doing whatever he wanted, certainly not his parents.

"College is like another universe," Ali said. "The boys are so wild. And the parties! Your silly SIGMA bashes don't come close, Spence."

Spencer had started a secret society called SIGMA, which threw floating parties known for their reckless abandon—drinking, gambling, hooking up, whatever. Students could gain entrance to the bashes only by exclusive invitation or by knowing that night's password. Trying to get into a SIGMA party was the goal of every high school student in North Jersey.

"SIGMA's getting hotter this year," Spencer vowed, sipping from his own tumbler of whiskey. "Bigger, too. I'm thinking of having a burlesque show, where the hotties of Hillsdale do a striptease—"

"Get over yourself, Spencer," Coco snapped. "No one's going to do a striptease at a SIGMA party."

"They will if they're drunk enough," Spencer said. "You've come close a few times."

Ali laughed and Coco scowled. "Please," Ali said. "That's baby stuff. Up at Yale we go out every night—the key is never to sign up for a class that meets in the morning. Some guy always has a keg going in his dorm suite, but I like the late-night cocktail parties better. There are these secret societies that, like, presidents and major business leaders have belonged to, and they have these elaborate club-houses that look like Greek temples, and you can't believe what goes on in there. They're all sworn to secrecy, but rumors do go around. . . ."

"I've already decided I'm going to pledge Skull and Bones when I get up there two years from now," Spencer said.

"You totally should," Ali said. "Then you can tell me all about it."

Coco rolled her eyes. "How are you going to get into Yale, Spencer? Your grades don't even come close to being good enough."

"Who needs grades?" Spencer said. "My mother is the new governor of New Jersey come January—or have you forgotten? That wouldn't be like you, Cocopuff, to forget something as important as that. Especially since you're so crazy about the thought of setting up camp in the governor's mansion."

Ali laughed. "You always were a suck-up, Coco. Come on, Spencer, make a bet or fold your pathetic little hand."

"I'm in for twenty," Spencer said. "So have you met any famous people's kids yet?"

"Are you kidding?" Ali said. "They don't let you in unless your parents are rich and/or famous or you're a genius."

"How'd you get in, then?" Coco asked, expressing exactly what Haley was thinking but was too polite to say out loud.

"Genius, of course," Ali said without batting an eyelash. "One of my suitemates, Carlotta, has a pied-à-terre across from the Met on Fifth Avenue. Her mother's a Spanish duchess or something—they're related to the Spanish royal family somehow—and she's never there, so Carlotta brings a gang of us down to the city to party in style all weekend . . . but I swear the best part is that nobody has to know where I am or what I'm doing. I don't have to check in with Mom or Consuela and lie to them about what I've been up to all night. I just love that freedom."

"When do you study?" Haley asked. "I mean, isn't Yale kind of a tough school? Don't you have a lot of work to do?"

"Work, shmerk," Ali said. "Read this, read that . . . you don't even have to show up to lectures if you don't feel like it. We get a week before exams to study—I'll make up all my work then."

"Really, why waste your time studying?" Spencer said. "You're young, you're beautiful—it's your time to live, baby!"

"Oh, Spencer, shut up," Coco said. "Can we talk about something else, please?"

"Like what, baby sis?" Ali said. "Homecoming? The latest zit creams?" She and Spencer snickered. Haley could feel Coco fuming beside her, probably because Coco's forehead was showing some signs of stress.

"You're hilarious," Coco snapped.

Haley decided to change the subject. "Did you guys hear that Reese Highland broke his foot in the soccer game today? He left the field on crutches."

"You're kidding," Spencer said. He seemed genuinely upset. "He actually broke his foot? Or just sprained something?"

"It's broken," Haley said. "My mother talked to his mother when they got back from the emergency room."

"That sucks," Spencer said. "Does this mean he won't be playing hoops this year?"

"Looks that way," Coco said, glad someone had finally snatched her boyfriend's attention away from her self-centered sister.

"But we need him." Spencer dropped his cards on the table and said, "I'm out." Then he got up, glass in hand, and paced the room. "This was going to be the year the Hawks go all the way! Without Reese it's going to be impossible—or close to it. . . ."

While Spencer muttered drunkenly about the fate of the basketball team, Haley's bag vibrated. She reached inside and pulled out her buzzing cell phone. A text was coming in—from Reese, of all people.

```
Need 2 C U. Meet me 4 a bite
at Hap's?
```

"What is it?" Coco leaned over, trying to read Haley's phone, which immediately vibrated again—another text coming in.

"Nothing, just a text," Haley said, glancing at the new message. This was from Sasha Lewis—a former sidekick of Coco's, now estranged.

```
The whole posse's going to
Bubbies,
```

the text said.

```
Come meet us!
```

"Now what?" Coco asked, her usual nosy self.

"Nothing," Haley said. "I'll be right back."

She got up and went into the bathroom. She needed a minute to think without Spencer and Ali's inane chatter cluttering her mind. If she went to Hap's to meet Reese, she didn't want Coco tagging along. And if she chose to go see Sasha and Whitney, they especially wouldn't appreciate Coco's presence. But if Coco knew where Haley was going, in either case, she might insist on tagging along. And it wasn't easy saying no to Coco—*no* was a word Miss De Clerq refused to hear.

● ● ●

With Ali around, Coco needs a friend, no question. She could use Haley's help—but does she deserve it? She's not exactly the most loyal, reliable friend to Haley. But maybe you think Haley is the type who rises above that,

who is good even to those who've wronged her. Or maybe you think everybody will feel a lot better once Ali is gone again—including Haley. Getting rid of Ali could make all their lives easier. And no one wants to see two sisters tear each other limb from limb—do they? If you think Haley needs to get Ali back to college quick, before she does anything else to harm Coco and Spencer's unstable union, turn to page 109 (SEND OFF ALI).

Maybe Haley should put as much distance between herself and the De Clerq sisters as she can and go hang with Reese. If you think Haley will take any chance she can get to be alone with Reese on a date, go to Hap's on page 106 (CASTAWAY). If you think Haley would rather go hang with Sasha, Cecily, Whitney and their boyfriends, go to Bubbies on page 122 (MAMMA MIA).

Of course, maybe you think none of those choices is right for our Haley. If you're not convinced she has any idea what to do with her social life, turn to page 101, FAMILY JEWELS. Sometimes the gem you've been waiting for is sitting right under your nose.

SISTERLY LOVE

There's always a story behind a girl with red eyes.

"H-A-W and K! We're the team to beat today! We don't care what others say—Hillsdale Hawks are on the way! Goooo, Hawks!"

Haley clapped and shouted along with the rest of Hillsdale High at the annual pep rally to kick off the basketball season. The basketball court was a sea of blue and gold. Cecily Watson glowed as she led the cheers, jumping up and down and revving up the crowd.

Sasha Lewis put two fingers between her lips and

let out a piercing whistle. "Woo-hoo! Go, Hawks! Go, Johnny!"

"Yeah!" Whitney Klein called. "Go, Johnny Lane!"

Haley smiled at Whitney's show of solidarity. Johnny Lane, one of the stars of the basketball team, was Sasha's boyfriend. Ever since Whitney and Sasha had been forced to spend Thanksgiving break together at their blended family's new house, they had been inseparable. They now rooted for the same players, wore the same clothes, listened to the same music and ate off each other's plates. Never mind that a year ago Whitney had turned up her nose at the sight of Sasha's boyfriend, the leather-clad rebel Johnny Lane, considering him her social inferior— or that he'd been no fan of Whitney's, either.

"How times change," Haley said to herself.

"What's that?" Whitney asked.

"Nothing." Haley enjoyed sitting with her friends, seeing them get along so well and feeling like they were all a part of the same group at school. The only distraction was Reese sitting courtside on the bench, dressed in button-down shirt and tie, his left foot in a cast, with crutches propped beside him. He clapped for the others, as Haley knew he would—he was nothing if not a good sport—but it had to be hard for a star forward to be sidelined with an injury and miss out on the whole season. Haley felt sorry for him. She could tell that even though he was trying to stay positive, he wasn't feeling like himself.

Once the cheerleaders had done their jobs, the team took the floor. Cecily and the rest of the squad sat down in the front row, right in front of Haley. Cecily turned around and beamed at her friends. "I can't wait to see Drew play again," she said. "I mean, I love him and all, but I'm aware that he's basically an ordinary guy—off the court. On the court he's like an animal—all instinct. *Grrrr!*"

Haley laughed and watched as Drew and Johnny warmed up by passing the ball quickly back and forth. "Too bad the third member of their starring trio is down for the count."

"Totally," Sasha said. "I don't know what they're going to do without Reese. When Johnny heard he was hurt, I think I saw him tear up."

"This was going to be their year," Whitney said.

"It still can be," Cecily said. "Come on, guys! This is a pep rally! Where's your team spirit?"

Sasha laughed. "I left it in my locker with my pep," she joked.

The team started scrimmaging. They looked good, Haley thought, but without Reese there was a gaping hole in the offense. A few of the seniors hustled, hoping to fill the gap, but they just didn't have that Reese magic.

Halfway through the first period, Mia Delgado walked into the gym.

"What cat dragged *that* in?" Sasha whispered.

Mia Delgado was a Spanish beauty who seemed

to be visiting Hillsdale on an extended visa. She was the ex-girlfriend of Sebastian Bodega, an exchange student from Spain. Sebastian was no slouch himself, with sexy brown eyes, wavy dark hair and broad shoulders—he was, after all, a star swimmer. But Mia looked like a supermodel: five foot ten, leggy, with lustrous dark hair and perfect bone structure. And, in fact, she had done her fair share of modeling, especially in Europe.

Mia squeezed her way through the mob of students and sat down in the bleachers one row behind Haley and her friends. Up close, Haley couldn't help noticing that Mia's eyes were red and bloodshot—not her usual look. Haley wasn't the only one who noticed.

"What do you think is the matter with her now?" Whitney whispered.

"Maybe she was out partying all night," Haley whispered back.

"It's got to be more than just that," Whitney said. "It looks more like she's been crying. But what on earth would Mia have to cry about? Her life is perfect!"

"Nobody's life is perfect," Haley said, though if Mia had any major problems, Haley didn't know about them.

"Maybe she's pregnant with Sebastian's love child," Whitney suggested.

"That is how rumors get started," Sasha warned.

As the game ended, Mia disappeared, seeming to melt into the crowd. "I guess the secret behind Mia's red eyes will have to stay a mystery," Whitney said. "For now, anyway."

"I'm starving," Sasha said. "Let's go to Bubbies and get something to eat."

"Sounds perfect," Whitney agreed.

"I'll go tell Drew and Johnny to meet us there," Cecily said, running off toward the locker room.

"You coming, Haley?" Sasha asked. "It'll be fun!"

Haley started to answer but stopped when Reese hobbled over on his crutches. "Hang on."

"Some scrimmage, huh?" Reese said, trying to sound cheerful.

"Well, they looked good, but not as good as when you're playing," Haley said supportively.

"Thanks," Reese answered, "but I think they'll be just fine without me. My work here is done. So you want to go to Hap's for a bite?"

Haley looked at Reese, who was leaning on his crutches and favoring his good right foot. He was probably tired from hobbling around all day— maybe he just wanted a quiet dinner alone with her. Which wouldn't be a bad thing at all. . . . She could always use more time alone with him.

On the other hand, he hadn't exactly made a lot of effort to fit her into his busy schedule lately. Reese seemed to expect her to jump when he called, but what about *her* social life? Maybe she should be more independent and do as she pleased—just the way Reese did.

● ● ●

Bistro fare or greasy comfort food? A quiet supper or a raucous get-together with friends? If you think what Haley and Reese need is a quiet night of down-home cooking at Hap's—just the two of them—go to page 106 (CASTAWAY).

Or would that be too quiet? Reese did seem a little bummed out after having to watch his team from the sidelines. Maybe Captain Bringdown needs some time to himself, and Haley needs a little fun with her friends. If you think Haley should hang with the girls and let Reese go home without her, go to page 122 (MAMMA MIA).

Lastly, if you think Haley should go home and call it a night, turn to page 101 (FAMILY JEWELS).

GARAGE BANDWIDTH

**Sometimes clutter hides
a world of pain.**

"**W**ait until you see the house," Annie Armstrong said as she led Haley up the steps to Mr. Von's front door. "Dave's mom has totally had her way with the place. Except for the garage—Mr. V declared the garage off-limits to all cleanup attempts."

Haley had reluctantly agreed to visit Annie's boyfriend, Dave Metzger, at his new house. Dave's mother had just moved in with their art teacher, Rick Von, at his littered bungalow near Hillside Heights. Dave's psyche was always in a fragile state, and Haley worried that a major change like this could push him over the edge. Annie insisted things were okay at the new Metzger/Von homestead and brought Haley along to see for herself. In any case, Dave was about to broadcast the next installment of his live video podcast, "Inside Hillsdale," and Haley wanted to watch behind the scenes and maybe even put in an appearance on air.

Annie rang the doorbell, which was shaped like a belly button. "I'm sure *this* is on its way out," she said. Dave greeted them sullenly.

"Hello," he said, scratching a patch of hives on his neck. "Welcome to my world."

He led them inside the craftsman-style abode. Haley had to admit that the house was surprisingly tidy and cozy—surely the work of Dave's mom. "We can skip this part," Dave said, waving his hand dismissively at the stairs leading up to the bedrooms. "There's nothing to see here."

As they slipped past the kitchen, Haley caught a glimpse of Dave's mom, Nora, vigorously scrubbing the pantry. "Hello there, kids," she called, waving one pink-rubber-gloved hand.

"Hello, Mrs. Metzger," Haley said.

"It never ends," Dave lamented, barely glancing at his mother. He led Haley and Annie out through a side door and into a place that wasn't tidy at all: Mr. Von's dingy garage. Haley thought it was actually kind of cool, in a funky, rustic sort of way. It was crammed with old records, stereo equipment, art supplies and Mr. Von's latest large, abstract paintings. In addition to all of that, Dave had his piles of books and software programs and his videocasting equipment.

"How about some John Coltrane?" Dave flipped through a stack of records and pulled out an old album. The music added to the funky, dusty atmosphere, Haley thought.

"This is where I come to get away from it all," Dave said. He nodded toward the house. "They're always . . . I can't even bring myself to say it."

"Making out," Annie said for him. "They're all over each other. It is truly disgusting."

"Just thinking about it keeps me up at night," Dave said. "I mean, even more than usual."

"That's terrible," Haley said. She felt for Dave, but secretly she also thought, *Good for them*. Why shouldn't Mr. Von and Mrs. Metzger be happy? Maybe Dave just needed to get used to the new arrangement.

But healthy adjustments were not Dave's forte. "I had another one of those dreams last night," he said. "You know, where I'm a lone voyager in space? Only this time I didn't even have a capsule. I was floating outside without my spacesuit, even though that's technically impossible to do without exploding out of your skin—"

"Poor Davy," Annie said dismissively.

She must get tired of hearing about all his phobias and weird dreams, Haley thought. *I certainly wouldn't be able to put up with it.*

"So Haley," Annie began, changing the subject, "have you heard about this new Web site at school? The one with all the scandalous rumors posted on it?"

Haley gave a clueless look.

"It's called Hillsdale Hauntings," Annie continued.

"No," Haley said. "I haven't heard of it."

"Supposedly they've even got videos of Hillsdale students in *compromising positions,* if you know what I mean," Annie added. "I've tried to check it out but the server's always busy or something—so it must be good, right?"

"Who've they got video footage of?" Haley asked innocently.

"Well, there are rumors flying that they've got Zoe Jones dancing around a stripper pole," Annie said. "No one told me if she takes anything off or not." Zoe Jones was a very pretty and talented sophomore who led a band called Rubber Dynamite. Because of her outrageous style, she was a frequent target of rumors, most of them untrue.

"I'd like to check it out for myself," Haley said. "Do you know the URL?"

"Sure," Annie said. "But I've heard you have to use a password to see the good stuff."

". . . I just wish I knew for sure whether those

blueberries had been washed before I ate them," Dave was muttering, scratching at his shirt sleeves. "I could have ingested tiny microscopic spiders—they burrow into your stomach lining and set up camp there for years, living off your undigested food."

"Ew," Haley said.

"I'm sure the blueberries were spider-free," Annie reassured him, patting Dave's hand.

"Mr. Von doesn't wash things like he should," Dave said. "I mean Rick. He said to call him Rick. But I still think of him as Mr. Von. What kind of father is that? Mr. Father? Where's my real father? I think I need to find my real father. That's it. My real father would never let me eat unwashed blueberries. Real fathers protect you from danger—"

"Shouldn't you get ready for your videocast, Dave?" Annie said. She turned on the large lamp he used for lighting when broadcasting.

"Do you think he should?" Haley whispered to Annie. "He seems even more anxious than usual."

"He'll be okay," Annie said. "Trust me, it's worse if he doesn't videocast. He needs to get this stuff out of his system."

"Yes. Yes. I'm ready. Ready for transmission," Dave said through clenched teeth. He turned on the video camera and aimed it at a stool in front of a backdrop made from an old sheet. Then he sat on the stool and cleared his throat.

"Welcome to this edition of 'Inside Hillsdale,'

coming to you from a not-so-secret location deep in the bowels of New Jersey's Bergen County."

Annie dropped her face in her hands. "Oh, brother."

"Tonight I have an important message for everyone out there in the land of the living," Dave said. "Somewhere in cyberland is the man who is my father. I don't know where he is or what he's doing now. But he's out there somewhere, maybe waiting for a signal from me that it's time to return. Dad, if you get this message, come back and rescue me! Before it's too late. And you, my dedicated and loyal viewers, I need your help. Please help me find my father. If any of you knows a Mr. Metzger, please contact me immediately through my Web site. And now, I'll share with you a song I heard while drifting through space in my dreams last night. *A-ohhhhh. A-ohhhh. Oh-eeee. Ee-aahhh . . .*"

Poor Dave, Haley thought. He was getting perilously close to his flat-out crazy place. Something had to be done. Haley just didn't know what.

● ● ●

Dave is getting weirder by the second. How does Annie handle it? She seems kind of oblivious, but there are signs she's aware of the trouble Dave's in and just isn't willing to face it. If you think Haley is the sympathetic sort who can't watch a sad display like this and not do

something to help a lost cause, turn to page 128 (SEARCHING FOR MR. METZGER).

Perhaps you think Haley feels sorry for Dave, but that he's beyond any help she can offer. Haley's strong artistic side is bound to be stimulated by being in her art teacher's house—even though the house has been sterilized by Mrs. Metzger. If you think all those canvases and jazz records in the garage are inspiring Haley to create art with a capital *A*, help her satisfy her jones by turning to page 137 (ART CLASS).

On the other hand, if all this weirdness is too much for Haley and you think she needs to decompress, turn to page 146 and let her spend some TIME ALONE. Finally, if you're curious to hear what the principal of Hillsdale High is ranting and raving about these days— always a clue to the latest school scandals—go to page 153 (PRINCIPAL CRUM'S LITANY).

There's all kinds of chaos in Hillsdale these days. But how much nuttiness can Haley take? That's up to you.

TAKE THE LEAD

Rejection is just a phone call away.

Just call him, Haley thought. *What have you got to lose?*

Her hand hovered over her cell phone. What *did* she have to lose? Only everything. Okay, not everything. Just her dignity, her pride and her ability to be in Devon's presence without feeling too unbearably weird. Her ambiguous sort-of friendship with Devon was, frankly, fraught with sexual tension, and calling him up and asking him out was a surefire way to make it even more awkward. Unless he said yes, which would present a different but better set of problems. She'd deal with those as they came.

Blah blah blah, she thought. *You always overthink things. Just get it over with!*

She grabbed the phone and dialed Devon's number before she had a chance to stop herself. He picked up on the third ring.

"Devon! Hi!" Her voice sounded too bright but she couldn't make it stop. "It's Haley."

"Haley—hey." Did she catch a hesitation in his voice? She couldn't tell whether he was glad to hear from her or not. He sounded . . . preoccupied. "So what's up?"

"Um, I was just wondering if you felt like catching a movie tonight," Haley said, clearing her throat. "Have you seen *Pardonnez-moi*? It's playing at the Rialto."

Devon didn't say anything for a few torturous seconds. Was he still there? Had he heard her?

"Devon?"

"Sorry. Hang on a sec." Haley heard a rustle, as if he was putting his hand over the phone, and his muffled voice speaking to someone in the room. He returned and stuttered, "S-sorry, Haley. Uh, I'd really like to go, but I can't."

Haley froze. She waited for more explanation, but nothing came.

Hello? Say something!

But he'd already said something. He'd said no. Now what should she do?

Abort! Abort! Get off the phone, quick!

"Okay, well, maybe some other time," she mumbled. "Bye!" She hung up and dropped the phone as if it had burned her fingers. How could she have been so stupid?

"I'd like to go, but I can't"? What did that mean?

What could Devon be so busy with that night? Haley knew Shaun and Irene were spending the evening at Shaun's house alone. Knowing Shaun, they were probably eating pudding off each other's stomachs or something equally bizarre.

So Devon should have been free, in theory. If he had something innocent to do, like watch his little sister, why didn't he just say so instead of acting all strangely about it?

She wondered who'd been in the room with him. That little blond neighbor of his, Darcy Podowski, perhaps?

Images flashed through Haley's mind: Devon and Darcy speeding away from school in his convertible, her bleached hair flying, the two of them laughing at one of their private jokes. What exactly was going on between them, anyway? Could Devon really be interested in a ditzy little freshman?

Why not? Haley thought. Even though freshmen looked like infants to her now, they were only two years younger. Lots of older boys went after the frosh meat. She'd never thought of Devon as that type, but then, how well did she really know him?

She groaned and rolled over on her bed. *Stupid stupid stupid!* If only she could take back the last five minutes and stop herself from making that phone call!

And we have art class together tomorrow, she thought. Devon was in her class, of course. Even if she wanted to avoid him, she couldn't. They'd have to sit together in that cramped studio, listening to Mr. Von's ramblings. Things would be superstrained between them now, all because she just had to ask out Devon. Great. Just awesome.

Way to go, Haley, she said to herself. *Way to go and wreck everything.*

● ● ●

Poor Haley. She was brave to take a chance, but sometimes risks don't pay off, and this looks like one of those unfortunate moments. Still, she doesn't know for sure that Devon blew her off for Blondie. Maybe he really does have to babysit and he was just embarrassed or forgot to mention it.

So what should she do now? If you think she should try to pretend everything is normal between her and Devon, go to ART CLASS on page 137 and act like nothing ever happened. That might work. Then again . . . if you think Haley is so embarrassed by Devon's turning her down that she can't face another human soul, spend some **TIME ALONE** on page 146 to get over the awkward feelings.

If you think what Haley needs now is a little excitement, a distraction, if you will, and you'd like to find out about Hillsdale High's latest scandal, turn to page 153 (PRINCIPAL CRUM'S LITANY).

No pain, no gain, as they say. Who knows, maybe things will work out for Haley after all—if she makes the right moves now.

FAMILY JEWELS

You can learn a lot from a family tree, and even more from heirloom jewelry.

Haley was sitting at her dresser brushing her hair when she got that feeling: the one where you know someone is watching you. She turned and caught her mother standing in the doorway, smiling in a gentle, rueful way that was not particularly characteristic of Joan Miller, environmental attorney-at-law—aka She Who Strikes Fear in the Hearts of Polluters.

"What?" Haley asked. "You're freaking me out."

"Well, it's just that you're going to be seventeen

in a few months," her mother began. "Sometimes I just can't believe it, that's all. Seventeen."

"Uh, yeah," Haley said. "That's what usually happens. After sixteen comes seventeen. Then eighteen, nineteen . . ."

"Don't be cranky." Joan came into the room and sat down on the bed. "I was just admiring my beautiful daughter. Is that so terrible?"

"No," Haley said. "It's not terrible. Just a little weird. Make that a lot weird. This isn't where you start talking about birds and bees and where babies come from, is it? Because we've had that conversation, like, eight times already."

Joan shook her head and smiled. "Now that you're getting older, I was thinking that you might want to borrow something of mine. Something special. Anything you want."

"Anything?" This offer caught Haley off guard. Joan sometimes tried to get Haley to dress more like her, so Haley was a little suspicious. Was this Joan's roundabout way of turning Haley into a Mom clone? All organic attire and hemp woven shoes?

"Sure," Joan said. "Clothes, shoes, jewelry, whatever you like. What's the good of owning some of the nice things I have if I hardly ever wear them? And then I thought you might enjoy them."

So it wasn't a trap after all. Joan was just being Nice Mom for a day. "Thanks," Haley said. She knew immediately what she wanted to borrow—a piece of jewelry. She didn't own much that was valuable herself; it might be fun to have something important to wear on a date or to a party. If she ever got one of those invitations again.

"Okay, jewelry," she told Joan, waiting for her mother to retract her generous offer.

"Be my guest. You know where to find it. Just let me know what you pick out—I'll be curious to see." And with that, Joan went downstairs to her study. Haley was amazed, walking the hall to her parents' bedroom. She found her mother's jewelry box on top of the antique highboy, just where it was supposed to be. Haley took it down and sat on her parents' bed. She opened the box and touched the aging green velvet lining. She used to love rummaging through her mother's jewelry when she was little, but she hadn't gone peering into this private collection in years.

She reached for a lock of long, straight auburn hair, tied with a ribbon. Spooky: a bit of Joan's old ponytail from her college days. Haley remembered her mother talking about how she'd let her hair grow all the way down to her butt back then. Then in college she'd cut it all off to donate to a wig drive for cancer patients. She'd never grown her hair past her shoulders again. Too girlish, she said.

Joan Miller was not a froufrou, frivolous woman, and she owned only five important pieces of jewelry. All five were wonderful, though. It wouldn't be easy to choose just one.

First Haley examined the large vintage cocktail ring with the rose-gold flower, a college graduation gift to Joan from her aunt Marion. It was beautiful, elegant, a little showy, a little old-fashioned, but in a good way. Then there was the platinum watch Gam Polly, Perry's mother, had given Joan as a wedding gift, with diamonds on the hands and on each hour marker. Next Haley tried on a stack of funky, bold Bakelite bracelets Joan had picked up in a vintage store in San Francisco. Then there were the classic pearl earrings—pearl studs with a larger pearl drop hanging from each—Joan's mother had given her for her high school graduation. Finally, Haley examined a gold and coral antique cameo brooch that Joan had inherited from her grandmother.

Haley wished she could borrow them all, but her mother had said just one, so Haley had a decision to make.

● ● ●

Help Haley decide which jewelry item to borrow. What kind of statement do you think she wants to make?

If you want her to pick the cocktail ring, go to page 170 (BOOB TUBING). If you think Haley will choose the platinum watch, go to LADY-IN-WAITING, page 161. To have her grab the Bakelite bracelets, send her to ART CLASS on page 137. To choose the pearl earrings, turn to page 128 (SEARCHING FOR MR. METZGER).

Or to pick the antique cameo brooch, go to page 178 (HOOP DREAMS).

Some people believe that objects have a karma of their own, which transfers from one owner to the next. For Haley's sake, let's hope the jewelry you picked brings good vibes her way.

At a romantic dinner for two, fifteen is a crowd.

"I'll get that." Haley darted in front of Reese, who was hobbling on his crutches, to open the door of Hap's Diner.

"Thanks." Reese looked embarrassed. "You know I'd open it for you if I could. Maybe after a few days, with a little more practice on the crutches—"

"Don't worry about it," Haley said. They walked into Hap's for their quiet dinner together, just the two of them. Reese had just broken his left foot, but Haley was hoping the injury would have an upside:

it might give him more time to spend with her. So far, things were working out exactly as she'd planned. If this kept up, she wouldn't mind opening doors for him all semester.

Hap's was busy that night. As Haley and Reese made their way to the hostess station, a hush fell over the room and heads turned to stare at Reese's cast. Haley recognized kids from school, neighbors, and people she didn't know but had seen around town in the year and a half since she'd moved to Hillsdale.

"What's their problem?" Haley said to Reese. "Haven't these people ever seen a foot in a cast before?"

Reese just shrugged and smiled. The hostess station was unattended, as usual; Hap saved money by letting the waitresses double as hostesses, and they were all busy that night. Reese spotted Hap manning the counter and gave him a wave. Hap wiped his hands on a dish towel and hurried over to greet them.

"Reese Highland!" Hap said. "Oh my goodness. What happened to you? Hillsdale's greatest soccer star! What will the team do without you?"

Reese looked down at his foot modestly. "It was so muddy out there, I got tripped up in the game and broke the thing. Nothing serious—"

"Nothing serious! Look at that cast! Come, I'll seat you myself." He stopped a passing waitress, saying, "I'm giving this couple table fourteen—the best booth in the house," he added to Reese. "You treat them good, hear?"

"Sure thing, Hap," the waitress said. "I'll be right over with your menus."

Tugging on his stained apron, Hap led them to a booth in the farthest corner of the restaurant. Haley could feel the eyes of the other diners on them. "Is this okay for you? Will you be comfortable here?"

"It's great, Hap," Reese said. "Thanks."

"My pleasure. Wait, I'll be right back."

The waitress delivered the menus, and Hap brought a small votive candle to the table and lit it.

"There. For you," Hap said. "I hope you enjoy your dinner."

"Thanks so much," Haley said, amazed at all the fuss.

"Yes, thank you, Hap. You really didn't have to go to the trouble," Reese said. "It's just a broken foot."

"Not just any broken foot," Hap said. "*The* broken foot! The most important foot in Hillsdale. Anyway, it's no trouble! Not for a five-time winner of the Hap's Challenge."

He disappeared into the kitchen. "I'll be back in a minute to take your orders," said the waitress, whose name tag read *Tara*.

"Well," Haley said, now that they were finally alone in their cozy booth. "This is nice."

"Very nice," Reese said, opening his menu. "Dinner's on me—get anything you like."

As Haley considered Greek salad and spinach pie, a shadow fell over the table. She looked up to see three Hillsdale students, two boys and a girl, probably sophomores, if she had to guess, staring down at them.

"Reese, dude, what the heck happened to you?" one of the boys asked.

"Did you get hurt real bad in the game?" the girl asked.

"Yeah," Reese said. "I was drilling toward the goal when one of the Old Tappan defenders fouled me. I tripped over his legs and broke my foot. Fell flat on my face, too. Covered in mud. The worst part is the ref didn't even call the foul."

"That sucks, man," one of the boys said.

"I wish I'd seen it," the girl said. "I wanted to go to the game but I couldn't because I had my elo-elo-elocution lesson."

The second boy stared at Reese's foot under the table. "Hey, dude—nobody's signed your cast yet. I want to be the first."

"Me too," the girl said. "Can I sign your cast, Reese?" She batted her big brown eyes.

"Sure, go ahead." Reese propped his foot on the booth seat while the girl pulled a purple gel pen from her pocket and started drawing hearts on Reese's cast. The boys signed *Stay tough* and *Hawks rule!* Tara the waitress returned to take their order, and borrowed the girl's pen to sign.

Even the waitstaff? Haley thought, aghast. *Okay, you've signed the cast, now leave us in peace.*

But before Haley and Reese had even finished ordering, another group of kids hovered near the table, waiting to talk to Reese. "Reese, man, what happened?"

"Old Tappan? We should go kick their asses!"

"No, no," Reese said. "That won't be necessary. This was all in the line of duty."

Oh, brother, Haley thought as he launched again into the story of how he broke his foot. She knew Reese was a local sports star, but she hadn't realized just how popular he really was.

By the time their food was ready, Tara had to fight through a crowd of admirers to deliver their plates, and Reese's cast was covered in ink. Haley stared at her salad and spinach pie, her appetite gone. So much for their romantic dinner alone— she'd barely gotten to say a word to him since they sat down. Meanwhile he had told and retold the story of his broken foot. Haley thought if she heard one more person say "What happened to your foot?" she'd scream—and possibly break Reese's other appendage for good measure.

Reese popped a french fry into his mouth and joked with his mob of admirers. He glanced at Haley, sitting glumly in front of her untouched plate.

"What's the matter? Don't you like what you ordered?" he asked her.

"No, it's not that," Haley said. "It's just—"

"Reese, is there any white space left on your cast for me?" a senior asked.

"Sure, I think we can find something. . . ." Reese pulled the leg of his jeans a little higher and scanned for an empty spot so that another girl could write her name. Haley felt sick.

"Hey, did you hear Spencer Eton is going to replace you on the hoops squad?" the senior flirt said.

Haley's ears perked up. Spencer Eton? Play a sport? She'd seen him shooting free throws in Reese's driveway, and he wasn't bad, but he wasn't exactly the disciplined, team-player type. Not to mention that his late-night carousing would never be allowed by even the most lenient coach. Haley wondered if the rumor was true.

Reese looked as if this was the first he'd heard of it. "Spence is a great player," he said. "The team could use him. I'm glad he's finally getting his head back in the game."

"Well, they need somebody," another senior said. "They'll be desperate now that you're out for the season." He signed his name with a flourish. "Thanks, man."

"No problem."

Haley's purse buzzed. She'd left her phone on Vibrate, not wanting anything to disturb her quiet moment with Reese. Now, she figured, what difference did it make? She pulled out her phone and, speaking of Spencer, found a text from Coco De Clerq.

"My birthday's coming up. Gov manse won't be ready till Jan. so we're doing it at chez De Clerq. But . . . Gov. Eton will be in attendance," the text said. "Want 2 help me plan? I've got to deal with invites and flowers and you have such a good eye. . . ."

Normally, the thought of helping Coco plan a major party in honor of herself gave Haley the shivers—but this was different. For one thing, at that moment Haley felt like leaping at any chance to get out of Hap's and away from Reese's adoring fans. For another, this wasn't going to be just any party. The new governor would be there, along with the crème de la crème of Hillsdale society—Coco was, after all, now the First Girlfriend. Haley wasn't sure which shocked her more: that Coco had invited her to the party at all, or the fact that Coco had kinda, sorta, almost said something nice to her.

"What is it?" Reese asked. "Something important?"

"Maybe," Haley said.

● ● ●

So much for a date with Reese—this felt more like a date with the entire town. Haley is getting fed up with Mr. Wonderful's inability to spare even a little time and attention for her. Between his academic ambitions and now his fan club, you can't blame Haley for looking for other ways to spend her time.

So what will it be? What's behind Coco's invitation to help plan her party? Is it sincere for once, or does the social queen of Hillsdale have a hidden agenda? To have Haley run errands with Coco, go to page 161, LADY-IN-WAITING.

If you think this disaster of a date has made Haley want to lock herself in her room and never come out, send her home for some TIME ALONE on page 146.

Maybe you think Haley wishes she'd gone to Bubbies Bistro with Sasha, Whitney and the gang instead of grasping at the hollow promise of alone time with Reese. If so, go over to Whitney's house and see some BOOB TUBING on page 170.

If you're worried about the basketball team and want to find out if the pampered Spencer has really signed on to replace the injured Reese, go to page 178 (HOOP DREAMS).

Finally, if you're ready to get Haley up to speed on what everyone else in town is talking about, go to PRINCIPAL CRUM'S LITANY on page 153.

You can't always get what you want—Haley knows that. But if you make the right choices for her now, she may end up with what she needs.

Sometimes getting rid of one problem just makes room for a new one.

"I love this time of year," Coco said. She and Haley sat in the back of the chauffeured SUV with Spencer and Ali, rolling down the West Side Highway toward Penn Station. The closer they got to seeing Ali off on the train to New Haven, the more Coco radiated relief, even joy. "I mean the time after Thanksgiving, when the Christmas decorations start to pop up everywhere. Of course, by the time Christmas vacation begins and people start coming home from college, the charm of the season has worn off. But now—these few short, happy weeks—I love them!"

Coco was clearly thrilled to be getting rid of Ali again. *Don't make it too obvious, Coco,* Haley thought, worried that Ali might suddenly decide to stay home and take the rest of the semester off if it meant messing with the head of her little sis. Spencer sat slumped in his seat, looking about as upset as Haley had ever seen him (which wasn't too terribly ruffled—he tended not to let much get him down). Ali seemed cranky about going back to school, too, in spite of all the wonderful things she'd said about it.

The car pulled up in front of the station, and the driver got out to open the back door and help Ali with her suitcase.

"Okay, then," Coco said, not leaving her comfy heated seat. "Bye, Ali! Have fun at school! See you at Christmas!"

"Aren't you going to come down to the train and see me off?" Ali snapped.

"I don't know about Coco and Haley," Spencer said. "But I'll see you off, Ali."

"Then we're going too," Coco said, pushing Haley out of the SUV. They left the driver with the car while Spencer rolled Ali's suitcase into the station, then went downstairs to the track where the train to Boston—with stops at all the usual places, including New Haven, Connecticut—sat waiting.

"Guess this is it," Spencer said, hugging Ali. "Hillsdale's so dull without you, Al. We'll party down heavily at Xmas."

"Abso-friggin-lutely," Ali said.

This hug was going on far too long for Coco's comfort level, so she inserted herself between her boyfriend and her sister. "Better get on the train, Ali. You're going to miss it."

"All right." Ali heaved her suitcase onto the train. "See you in a few weeks." She waved at all of them, but her eyes were trained on Spencer. The bell rang and the doors closed.

"Here's a hanky." Coco tossed Haley a silken square. "Wave goodbye." The train pulled away, and Coco nearly screamed, "Goodbye! Goodbye! And don't come back!"

"Coco, that's not nice," Spencer said. "Your own sister . . ."

Coco put on a fake sad face. "I'll miss her, I really will."

"Now you're just being sarcastic," Haley said.

"If she's my own sister, she ought to act like it," Coco said. "Besides, if college is so much frickin' fun, let her stay there. Let's go, Haley. We've got tons of errands to do back in town."

"We do?" Haley said. This was the first she'd heard about it. Typical Coco, to just assume Haley would be at her beck and call without even asking. Still, what choice did Haley have? She was in the city now, and Coco was her ride home.

"Yes, we do," Coco said. "My birthday is coming up, in case you forgot, and my party is going to be the most amazing bash in the history of Hillsdale. I was hoping to have it at the governor's mansion, but there's some silly little rule barring occupancy before the inauguration in January. So my parents are throwing a tea on our lawn. Governor Eton and several other state officials will be in attendance. So, I'll need your help with the preparations."

"A tea in December?" Haley asked, taking this all in. "And the governor?"

"Duh. Yes, of course. She is practically my mother-in-law. And don't worry, we're bringing in enough heat lamps to give everyone a sunburn. We've got to hit the stationer's first, then the florist, and I haven't bought a dress yet, so we might look at a few if we have time. . . ."

They rode the escalator back up to street level and got back into the waiting SUV. Spencer was busy with his high-speed PDA. He looked at Haley and smirked.

"Ugh, you're not on that stupid site Hillsdale Hauntings, again, are you?" Coco asked, clearly annoyed.

"What's Hillsdale Hauntings?" Haley asked innocently.

"Oh, you'll find out soon enough," Spencer replied.

"It's just some stupid Web site," Coco explained, "that's supposedly posting risqué videos of girls in our grade. I don't even know if I'm on it, nor do I care!"

Probably, Haley thought, guessing that there were quite a few people out there who might wish Coco De Clerq harm. She tried to imagine what it would be like to have embarrassing footage of yourself out there on the Web, but then thought, *Oh, silly, what have you ever done that could make Internet headlines?* Still, now that practically everyone had camera phones, you never knew when someone might snap an unflattering picture, or worse, video.

"You need some kind of secret password to get to see the good stuff," Spencer added.

"Secret password?" Haley said. "Isn't that kind of like your specialty, Spencer?"

"Yeah, you're the king of secret passwords," Coco said. "I'm sure you'll have it cracked within the hour. And anyway, how do we know that you're not the one behind Hillsdale Hauntings in the first place?"

Spencer smirked. "We don't."

"Well, when you get the password, call me," Coco said. "And promise not to look at it without me?" She bit her lip and batted her eyes, a move Spencer had never been able to resist.

He put his arm around her. "I promise I'll share the password with you as soon as I get it."

"Lovely. I've been waiting for a good scandal," Coco added. "Hillsdale's been so boring lately."

"Well, ladies," Spencer announced, looking at his watch, "much as I'd love to follow you around like a lapdog carrying all your stuff, I don't have time today. I've joined the basketball team, so I thought I better run a few laps or something before my first practice next week."

Coco's pretty little mouth fell wide open. "What? You what?"

Haley understood Coco's astonishment. The idea of Spencer playing a team sport—and taking it seriously—somehow did not compute.

"Since Highland is out for the season, I figured the team could use me," Spencer said with a shrug.

Coco laughed, a brittle, piercing sound. "Okay, I get it. You're joking, right? You're on the basketball team. Ha-ha. Now can we get back to planning my party?"

"I'm not kidding," Spencer said, and Haley could tell he was dead serious. "I'll be kind of busy, since I've got practice every day after school."

"Practice?" Coco said, still clearly having trouble believing this. "Every day? But . . . what about me?"

"I'll still see you plenty, honeybunch. Just not as much." Spencer tweaked her ear playfully. Coco glared at him, clearly not in the mood.

"What? Aren't I allowed to have a life too?"

"I thought you had a life," Coco said. "With me."

"Well, now it'll be even better," Spencer said. "Come on, it'll keep things interesting between us. We can't spend all of our time together."

Coco turned to Haley. "This all sounds very familiar to me." Coco was thinking of Reese's desappearing act, and Haley read her mind.

"See you ladies later," Spencer said, hopping out.

"Guess it's just you and me now, babe," Coco announced. "We'll get more done this way. Now for the invitations. Letterpress? Calligraphy?"

Haley shivered slightly at that thought. Since when had she become Coco De Clerq's gofer?

● ● ●

So, Spencer playing hoops. Practicing every day, running laps, maybe even giving up drinking . . . Is this for real? Spencer is putting on a pretty convincing act if it isn't. Now Coco will find out how Haley feels, always wondering when Reese will make time for her. Chances are Coco is not going to like it one bit, and when she suffers, everyone suffers. If you think Haley should check out Spencer's ball-handling skills, go to page 178, HOOP DREAMS.

Next shocker: the racy videos of Hillsdale High juniors. You know Spencer is all over that like white on rice. Or brown on rice, if you're a healthy eater like Haley. Whose little tushy could be on that Web site? If you think Haley would like some TIME ALONE to check out the site in the privacy of her own home, go to page 146.

If you think she'd rather hear more about the school's reaction to the scandal, go to **PRINCIPAL CRUM'S LITANY** on page 153.

Shopping with Coco might not usually be Haley's idea of a good time, but there are exceptions in play here. For one thing, Coco has an unlimited budget, which makes shopping a whole lot more fun. For another, if Haley tags along, maybe she can influence the direction this megabash takes. If you think she can't resist playing personal assistant, go to page 161 (**LADY-IN-WAITING**).

What with upheaval on the basketball team, the party of the year and the latest Web scandal, things are heating up in Hillsdale. How could Coco say the place is boring? The key to navigating these rocky shoals without getting hurt: making smart choices. Haley's role in all this is in your hands. Choose wisely.

Melted cheese and emotional meltdowns: perfect together.

Haley bit into her gooey turkey-Gruyère-and-arugula panino as Sasha swiped one of her french fries. Haley had met up with Sasha, Johnny, Cecily, Drew and Whitney at Bubbies Bistro, and she was glad she had. The kids were flying high after the basketball pep rally, in spite of the fact that with their star forward, Reese, injured and out for the season, the team would have to struggle to beat their closest rivals. Johnny and Drew played varsity hoops, and Cecily was captain of the cheerleading squad, so they all had a lot riding on Reese, though none of them as much as Haley.

"Who would've thought Spencer Eton would come to the rescue," said Johnny Lane, rubbing the dark stubble on his chin in annoyance. Johnny worked part-time as a busboy at Bubbies but was off that night. It wasn't his first choice as a hangout, but then Bubby never let him pay for his food.

"What are you talking about?" Whitney asked.

"Spencer just joined the varsity basketball team," Drew explained. "He wants to help out now that Reese is sidelined. Wonder how Coco is going to handle that news, especially when she was relying on him to plan her birthday tea with the gov."

"You have got to be kidding me," Sasha said, slinging an arm over Johnny's shoulder. "Is Spencer good enough to play varsity? Remember freshman year, when he quit the team before the first game?"

"We'll see," Drew said. "The coach must have thought he had the right stuff. He does possess a wicked hook shot."

"But that's pickup ball," Johnny countered. "Game play is a whole other story. It's different when you've got a rival team breathing down your neck, and not just one of your buddies. Spencer's a ball hog, plain and simple. He doesn't know how to play with a team."

"Give him a chance," Cecily chimed in. "Maybe being part of a team is exactly what Spencer needs to . . . I don't know . . . turn himself into a better person."

Haley nodded in agreement, then flushed, feeling silly and Pollyanna-ish. She really did believe a little discipline couldn't hurt him. She'd heard his grades had improved, and that was already a step in the right direction.

Sasha laughed. "Spencer, a better person? It's going to take a lot more than a little b-ball to accomplish that."

"Yeah, Spencer's got a ways to go before he picks up any philanthropy awards," Drew said. "He told me about this new Web site called Hillsdale Hauntings—have you guys seen it? It's supposed to be pretty hot." He glanced briefly in Haley's direction, then quickly looked away. *What was that about?* Haley wondered.

"People post pictures and videos of chicks from our school." Again Drew's eyes darted over to Haley, who dropped her sandwich and shifted uncomfortably. She didn't like those quick glances, but she couldn't be sure what they meant—and she was afraid to ask.

"Like who?" Whitney said.

"Like . . . Mamma Mia over there." Now Haley followed Drew's eyes to the corner booth, where Mia Delgado sat with a slick, older-looking guy, who was wearing a black turtleneck sweater, black pants and stylish black glasses. Mia herself looked stunning and chic in boots, a pencil skirt and a low-cut V-neck sweater. They'd huddled in the booth all evening, talking intently in low tones. Haley wondered who the man was and what Mia was doing with him. But then Mia's past was so checkered and glamorous, anything was possible.

"There's also some footage of other people we know," Drew said—again with the look in Haley's direction. Johnny coughed and added, "Boob tubing" under his breath. At least, that was what Haley thought she'd heard.

"What was that?" Haley asked.

Sasha shot Johnny a strange glance. "Oh, nothing," Johnny said.

Haley had the uncomfortable feeling that she'd missed something—that Johnny had made a reference that just flew completely over her head. Something was going on, and she wasn't sure she wanted to know what it was.

Suddenly a sob came from the corner booth. Mia ran past their table in tears and dashed into the ladies' room. The man in black stood up and stormed out of the restaurant looking highly pissed off. Haley and everyone else at the table craned their necks to watch him hop into a sports car parked in front of the restaurant and race away.

"What was that all about?" Sasha said.

"Hey, Mike." Johnny called over one of his coworkers, the waiter who'd handled Mia's table. "Who was that guy?"

"Just a sec." Mike swiped the check off Mia's table and glanced at the name on the credit card slip. "Philip Fogelman."

Whitney nearly jumped out of her seat. "Philip Fogelman! The fashion photographer?"

Mike the waiter double-checked the name and shrugged. "Yeah, I guess."

"I love his work!" Whitney blurted out. "He's so cutting-edge! I wish I'd recognized him sooner. I would have gone over to say hello or something."

"I think he was a bit *preoccupied*," Haley said. "Judging from Mia's meltdown."

"Well I can't stand his ad campaigns," Sasha said. "They're so perverse. What's the point?"

"I wonder if he has anything to do with the videos of Mia on that Web site," Cecily said.

"There's only one way to find out—watch the footage," Johnny suggested.

"Man, I've got to get on that site," Drew added, shaking his head.

● ● ●

For a fun night out with friends, this one has ended with a lot of drama. What was Mia doing with a big time photographer, in Hillsdale? And why was she crying? Even more mysterious is this Hillsdale Hauntings Web site.

Who's on it? Why did Drew keep looking at Haley? And what was with Johnny's cryptic "boob tubing" comment? Is there something on the site Haley should know about? Or maybe it's something she'd be better off not knowing about. As Johnny says, there's only one way to find out. If you think Haley's dying to see the Web site everybody's talking about, go over to Whitney's house and search the Web on page 170, BOOB TUBING.

If you're more curious to hear the school administration's reaction to the latest online scandal, turn to page 153, PRINCIPAL CRUM'S LITANY.

Speaking of drama, now that Whitney and Sasha are acting like the closest of sisters, what's their former leader, Coco, up to without them? Does she have any friends left? Who's going to help her plan her magnificent seventeenth-birthday-party tea with the governor now that Sasha, Whitney and Cecily are out of the picture? And meanwhile, who throws an outdoor tea in December? If you think Coco needs help with the party, and that Haley's just the girl for the job, go assist the LADY-IN-WAITING on page 161.

Finally, if you want to see how the Hillsdale Hawks play with Spencer on the team instead of Reese, go to HOOP DREAMS on page 178.

SEARCHING FOR
MR. METZGER

**If orange plastic cones
were an endangered
species, Annie Armstrong
would kill them off
for good.**

"Careful, careful . . ." Haley couldn't help quietly coaching Annie from the sidelines during the over-achiever's final driver's ed lesson. Annie was a few dozen yards away, with her teacher beside her in the passenger seat. She jerked the student-driver car into position to practice parallel parking. The windshield wipers suddenly came on, fluid squirting over the windshield.

Oops. Haley doubted Annie had meant for that to happen, on such a crisp sunny day. Every time

Annie went for the turn signal, something else happened.

"I don't know if she's ready," Haley confided to Dave Metzger, who stood beside her in the school parking lot, supposedly watching his girlfriend's driving lesson but actually more caught up in the information flashing from his handheld Web device. "She's going to the DMV next week, you know."

"A whole week," Dave said spacily. "That's plenty of time to master the fine art of piloting a motor vehicle through the streets of America."

"Not for Annie," Haley said. "Look—she's going for it."

"Uh-huh." But Dave's eyes were still glued to his handheld. He was currently sifting through every possible missing-persons database and identity-search site for some sign of his father. Finding his real dad was Dave's new obsession—actually the word *obsession* could not begin to describe the lengths Dave could go to when he had a problem to solve. It was more like a suicide mission. He was the most obsessed, well, *obsessive* Haley had ever known.

"Hey, look at this," Dave said, leaning toward Haley to show her the small screen in his hand.

Haley stared at the images for a second before they began to make sense. Then she recognized the video immediately: it was a home movie of Haley, age ten. She knew this clip all too well—in it, she rode on an inner tube pulled by a speedboat, laughing and happy, until the tube hit a wave and it knocked off her bathing suit. The boat sped on while Haley, screaming in embarrassment, was pulled along after it, half-naked.

"Oh my God," Haley muttered, horrified. "I can't believe this! Dave, where did you find this video?"

"On Hillsdale Hauntings," Dave said, referring to the site everyone had been talking about lately. Who needed a gossip column in the school paper when you could post dirt on a blog anonymously, far from the prying eyes of teachers, parents and Principal Crum?

Haley was in full panic mode. "How did it get out?" she shrieked. "How many people do you think have seen this?" And that's when she remembered her father's most recent project: archiving the Miller family home movies and transferring everything to digital at a local post house, for easier storage and access. And guess who was assisting him on the job: the class cutup and skatehead Garrett "the Troll" Noll.

"Judging from the number of downloads you've gotten, I would say . . . a lot," Dave replied.

Haley was mortified. Dave Metzger and who knew who else had now seen her naked. It was her younger, predeveloped naked self, of course, but it was still Haley. *However long it takes,* she silently vowed, *I am going to get back at Garrett for doing this. When he least expects it, I'll be waiting.*

"Uh-oh," Dave blurted out. "I think we might have an even bigger problem on our hands." Haley glanced up as Annie awkwardly began to back her car into the space between two parked cars—one of which was a shiny black sedan that just happened to belong to Principal Crum. Annie's car lurched backward, heading straight for a collision with Principal Crum's front bumper. "I can't watch." Dave covered his eyes.

At the very last second, Annie slammed on the brakes and screeched to a halt. Her car just barely kissed Principal Crum's, leaving only the very faintest of marks. Just then, Shaun Willkommen jogged by, waving at Haley. "No time to stop," he shouted. "I'm off to get *Deoottat*!"

"What?" Haley said.

"Deoottat," Shaun repeated, showing off his ability to speak backwards. Haley still hadn't mastered the art of deciphering this special Shaun language. "Come watch me mutilate my skin. It'll rock."

Now Haley understood what he meant: tattooed. Without giving Haley a chance to answer one way or the other, Shaun dashed over to Devon's beat-up convertible, which was waiting for him, engine running, in the junior parking lot. The top was up, so Haley couldn't quite make out who else was in the car, but she wondered with a twinge of jealousy whether

Devon's perky blond neighbor Darcy Podowski was riding shotgun.

"I wish that kid would say everything backwards all the time," Dave said, still tapping his computer with his thumbs.

"Why?" Haley asked.

"So I wouldn't have to know what he's saying," Dave said, trembling, before whispering, "He frightens me."

Annie got out of the student-driver car and ran over to hug Haley and Dave. "My last lesson! Thanks so much for waiting for me, you guys."

"No problem," Haley said. "Way to, uh, drive, there, Annie."

"What did you think, Dave?" Annie asked. "Am I ready for the DMV?"

"I thought you handled that car like a professional stock car racer."

"Really?" Annie said.

"Yeah, really?" Haley echoed.

"Yllaer," Dave said, imitating Shaun's backwards style.

"Wait a second," Annie said. "If you say 'really' backwards, does that mean you meant the opposite of *really*?"

Haley thought she ought to put a stop to this logic-fest before it got out of hand. "I think Dave was just copying Shaun—and when Shaun speaks backwards he doesn't mean the opposite of what he's saying. So I'm sure Dave was totally sincere."

"Yllatot," Dave said.

"Don't start that, Dave," Annie said. They all walked across the parking lot toward the main school building. "One backwards speaker at Hillsdale High is enough. So Haley, guess what!"

"What?"

"You're never going to believe it."

"Try me," Haley said, only half interested. She couldn't get the horror of that video, or her rage at the Troll, out of her mind.

"I got an invitation to Coco De Clerq's birthday party!" Annie nearly shrieked. "It's a tea at the De Clerqs', on the lawn! The governor will be there!"

Haley was of course invited to Coco's party too, but she had been afraid to mention it to Annie, who was perpetually barred from all Coco functions and had been for over a decade. Haley wondered how Coco could have had such a drastic change of heart. Was she just inviting everyone in their class? And if so, why would the Queen of Mean be so uncharacteristically nice to a longtime frenemy? "Isn't your birthday the same day as Coco's?" Haley pointed out. "And anyway, who wants to sit outside for three hours in New Jersey in December?"

"I'm sure, knowing Coco, it will feel like the tropics," Dave sighed.

"I don't see why any of that should stop me," Annie protested.

"I don't know, Annie—"

"Don't you have your driver's test booked for that day?" Dave interjected.

"Yes, Dave, I was planning to take my driver's test on my actual seventeenth birthday," Annie said. One of the quirks of living in New Jersey was a driving age of seventeen, instead of the usual sixteen. Haley could hardly stand to think of it. If she still lived in California, she could have been driving for nearly a year already. "But—"

"You would consider blowing off your driver's test just to go to a stupid birthday party?" Dave said. "And Coco's, at that—a girl who hasn't exactly been kind to you over the years?"

"I have my reasons."

"Your driver's test is way more important, Annie," Haley advised. "It's not easy to get an appointment at the DMV. You might have to wait weeks before another slot opens up."

"I know," Annie said defensively. "But don't you know what kind of opportunity this is? When else will I be able to corner the governor on her environmental policies? This is my one and only chance at a real tête-à-tête."

"I highly doubt that." Dave scoffed. "Do you really think the governor will want to talk business, if she even shows? Or that her security detail will let you near her if you so much as whisper a word about global warming? Besides, you won't exactly be able to present your case very well when it's forty degrees and you're shivering your butt off."

Annie frowned, considering Dave and Haley's points. Begrudgingly, she said, "You're probably right. The driver's test is more important."

For Haley, of course, the answers wouldn't be so simple. A terrible humiliation from the past had come back to haunt her. She realized she'd have to make the same decision as Annie: to go or not to go to Coco's major bash. Could she prove to the world that no silly little scandal would send her to hide under her bed? Or was she too embarrassed to make a public appearance now that everyone at school could see her naked, online?

She glanced around the parking lot and noticed a group of boys clustered by a car, pointing at her and whispering. Just then, a trio of freshmen walked by and giggled at the sight of her. This, Haley was sure, was just a taste of things to come.

● ● ●

So the mystery of the raunchy Web site is solved: one of the girls baring all is our little Haley! True, she was a flat-chested ten, but that's almost worse. If you think Haley is going to sprint home and hide under her covers, go to page 220, TOTAL MORTIFICATION.

Coco's not exactly loaded with talent, but one

talent she certainly has is the ability to stir things up and put people into quandaries. Haley sincerely believes that Annie should celebrate her own birthday by getting her driver's license—and not by kowtowing to the First Girlfriend of New Jersey. But does that mean Haley has to miss the party of the year too? How much sacrifice does friendship require? Does doing the right thing for a friend mean missing out on all the fun yourself? Complicating matters, what if Annie needs Haley's support at the DMV? And what if Annie decides to celebrate her birthday on her own—and has no one to celebrate with, because everyone else is at Coco's?

To have Haley stick with Annie for moral support on her birthday, and maybe even give her a few much-needed last-minute parallel parking tips, go to BUMP AND GRIND on page 185. To ditch Annie for Coco's sure-to-be-decadent birthday gala, turn to page 201, TEA AND SYMPATHY. Finally, if you think Haley should skip the birthday pressure altogether and run off to the TATTOO PARLOR with Shaun, Irene and Devon, go ahead to page 192.

To hide or not to hide? To party or not to party? To tattoo or not to tattoo? So many questions, so little time. Haley can't do everything, can't be everywhere. It's up to you to send her off in the right direction.

**The more freedom
you have, the easier it is
to screw up.**

Haley noticed something different the minute she sat down at her usual table for art class. First of all, there was Mr. Von himself. Dressed in a crisp, ironed button-down shirt, his pants pressed, his hair clean and combed, his stubbly beard trimmed, he looked like a different person, certainly not the mumbling, nutty art maniac Hillsdale students were used to. His desk, formerly a war zone of papers and books, was incredibly tidy and—shocker—the wood surface even had a waxy shine to it. In fact, the whole art room looked as if Mary Poppins had dropped in by umbrella and taken a broom to the place.

"Acid Rick's new live-in love must be implementing some serious reforms in the personal hygiene department," Irene Chen whispered.

"You know it," Haley said. "I just can't decide if it's a good thing or a bad thing."

"I'm leaning toward good thing," Irene said.

As the bell rang, Johnny Lane and Devon McKnight drifted in and sat with Haley and Irene at their table. Shaun Willkommen was in their art class too, but lateness was a habit with him, so Haley didn't think much of the fact that Mr. Von started the class without him.

"All right," Mr. Von rasped in his soft voice. "Let's settle down. Don't worry, I won't make you do anything hard today. I just want you to relax and lose yourselves in your own private worlds. We'll have a nice, easy free draw. It's a lesson in artistic license and self-motivation. Total freedom is not as easy to handle as some people think, you know. It can be a terrible burden, and that's why you all need to learn how to handle it. . . ."

Just then, the door burst open and Shaun barreled in stomach-first, holding aloft a stiff piece of stationery. "Ladies and germs, ladies and bacteria, ladies and streptococci," Shaun said, waving the paper over his head like a trophy and speaking in his best fake-Elizabethan accent. "It's here! It's here. The queen has spoken. I hold in my very hand an invitation to the seventeenth birthday party of one Miss Coco De Clerq. Oh yes! I do not lie. This is the genuine article. Perhaps you would like to gaze upon it?"

He waved the invitation under the noses of some laughing students. Haley recognized it immediately, since she'd just received one herself in the mail. Mr. Von sat calmly behind his desk, allowing Shaun to express himself by dominating the class.

"The queen has deemed me, young Master Shaun Willkommen, worthy of attending her fete, worthy of existing in her royal presence. What an honor, I say to you, ladies and gentlemen!"

"Lucky you," Johnny said sarcastically.

"Oh yes! Oh yes! I am indeed a fortunate lad," Shaun said. "This is the crowning achievement of my young life. The happiest moment I have ever known. For I would love nothing better on this earth than to celebrate Miss Priss's trip through the birth canal"— Shaun took a long pause—"*not!*" The class burst into laughter again. "Indeed, the only thing royal about Mademoiselle De Clerq is the royal pain she gives me in my arse!" Shaun brayed like a donkey, and Irene flinched. In the recent school production of *A Midsummer Night's Dream*, Shaun had played Nick Bottom, a weaver who is turned into a donkey-headed creature by a fairy. He'd taken the tenets of Method acting to heart—be the character, live the role at all times—and Irene was still recovering from the embarrassment of dating a guy who thought he was part mule.

"Sit down, Shaun," Irene snapped. "The only reason Coco invited you to her stupid party is because she wants something from you, or your parents."

"What say you, vile woman?" Shaun flared his nostrils to simulate outrage. "The Honorable Coco is only using me? But . . . that cannot be!" He clutched his heart and staggered as if the very thought of Coco's selfishness were mortally wounding him. The class was in an uproar.

"Please sit down, Shaun," Mr. Von said quietly, struggling to regain control. "Let's all settle down. We're exercising our freedom, but we musn't forget our self-discipline."

Shaun sat down next to Irene. "What's he talking about? What are we supposed to be doing?"

"Free draw," Haley told him.

"Awesome," Shaun said. "In other words, free-for-all."

"Exactly," Johnny said.

"I'm going to draw myself a tattoo," Shaun said. "And you're all welcome to do the same."

"Thanks for giving me permission, your lordship," Irene replied, her voice dripping with sarcasm.

They gossiped and talked while they worked on creative tattoo ideas. Haley had always vaguely liked the concept of a butterfly and started outlining one in colored pencils, even though drawing was not necessarily her forte. When it came to art, she was more of a film and photography girl.

Haley glanced across the table at Devon, who seemed very intent on his drawing. She tore her eyes away before he could catch her looking. Things had been a little awkward between them lately, and she didn't want to make the situation worse.

"I've always wanted an armband tattoo," Irene said. She showed her design, a circle of red ribbon intertwined with silver barbed wire. It expressed her pointed-yet-loyal personality perfectly. Off to the side she'd doodled an octopus with wavy arms.

"That's amazing," Haley said. She shaded her butterfly drawing with her hand. It looked pathetic next to Irene's designs.

"I like that octopussy over there," Shaun suggested.

"That's just a doodle," Irene said.

"Still, it rocks," Shaun said.

"There are so many things I'd like to try," Devon mused. "Here's the latest." His drawing was beautiful: a sweet-looking fish with shimmery blue, silver, pink, purple and gold scales.

"You'd have to find a really talented tattoo artist to do that right," Irene said.

"Do you know one who works pain-free?" Devon asked.

Johnny's dream tattoo was a flaming heart. "I've already got a few tats," he said, lifting his shirt and showing off two tropical flowers printed on his impressive washboard abs. "A big one like this would have to go on my back, I guess, and I'm just not sure I'm ready to make that major a commitment."

"I'm ready," Shaun said, waving his elaborate drawing of an orange and black tiger. "This is no hypothetical dream tattoo. This one's going to end up right here"—he pulled down his pants and mooned the class, slapping the paper against the skin on his buttocks. The class roared with laughter.

Mr. Von came over to their table to calm things down. "Shaun, let's wait to reveal the posterior after you've gotten the tattoo," he said. Haley supposed it was Mr. Von's strange way of being reasonable. "Until then, it's pants on."

Shaun pulled up his jeans. "Got it, Rickster. That's fair. But you're all on notice—prepare yourselves! What creature emerges when the tiger meets the ass?"

"That's one of those unanswerable questions," Johnny said.

"For sure," Irene said. "Haley, what's your tattoo?"

Haley looked down at her sad little butterfly sketch. Transferring it into permanent body art would be a major mistake. Everyone else's drawings were so much better. "I'm still working on mine," she said, folding up her piece of paper.

"Well, you better hurry up and finish," Shaun said. " 'Cause we're all going to the tattoo parlor and getting these babies inked up this afternoon!"

"Why don't you get a tattoo of an inner tube?" Johnny suggested with a snicker.

"What?" Haley said. She looked up, worried. She had no idea what he was talking about, but she didn't like the sound of his laughter.

"You know, because you're such a good tuber," Johnny said. Shaun was laughing now too, but Johnny stopped when he saw the clueless look on Haley's face. He shook his head. "Oh, no. You don't know, do you?"

"Know what?" Haley said, panic rising in her throat.

"About the video," Shaun said. "Online. Of you."

"What video?" Haley's voice was getting shrill.

"Hillsdale Hauntings," Shaun said. "That new Web site everybody's talking about. I have to say it is totally awesome."

"What are you talking about?" Haley said, but she was getting a very bad feeling. She'd heard people mention some raunchy Web site but she never seriously thought it could have anything to do with her. . . .

"It's an old home video of you from when you

were around ten," Johnny explained. "You're riding on an inner tube being pulled behind a motorboat, and . . ."

Haley didn't have to hear the rest. She knew what was coming.

"You hit a wave or something and your bathing suit comes off." Johnny paused while Shaun laughed harder, trying to hold it in, pounding a fist on the desk. "So basically you're, you know, naked. . . ."

Haley's face flamed red. *He can't mean this,* she thought. *He's teasing me. He heard about this old video somehow and decided to play a joke on me.*

"News *flash*. News *flash*. News *flash*," Shaun chanted, pounding his fists on the desk. Irene didn't crack a smile; she just kept on drawing, as if she were afraid to look up. Devon somehow avoided glancing at her, but Haley could tell this conversation had made his ears perk up. "I've seen it too."

No, Haley thought. *This isn't happening.*

It's all true? Johnny and Shaun and who knows who else have all seen me . . . naked?

● ● ●

This doesn't look good. There's still a chance Johnny's making up this story about a naked Haley online, but it's looking like this is for real. If you think Haley is dying of humiliation and can't think about anything but how this video will ruin her life, send her home screaming to see if it's true on page 220 (TOTAL MORTIFICATION).

Maybe you think Haley would seriously consider getting a tattoo after hearing there's a video of her in the buff circulating online. Hey, maybe she's feeling reckless, like, what's the difference now that everyone in school has seen her naked anyway? If so, send her to the TATTOO PARLOR on page 192.

If you think Coco's birthday party is a good chance for Haley to prove that some silly video won't get her down, go to page 201, TEA AND SYMPATHY. The event is sure to be amazing, at the very least—if Haley can stand the public scrutiny.

Just how brave is our Haley? Will she hide out in her room or face the possible scandal like a trouper? The after-shocks will depend on what you decide.

TIME ALONE

**The past is much more
likely to come back
to haunt you if you film it
on Super 8.**

Haley escaped to her bedroom and logged on to her computer. She was long overdue for some "one on none" time. Between all the drama in her life and the scandalous talk circulating at school, she needed to clear her head.

Once the door was closed, she took a deep breath and relaxed. From her bedroom window she could see the Highlands' driveway, but luckily there were no distracting signs of Reese. Now that his foot was broken, he was housebound, and it helped clear Haley's mind not to have him in view.

Haley checked her in-box and found an e-mail from Coco De Clerq with a link to a Web site for the teen queen's seventeenth birthday party. Haley clicked on it and a beautiful Web page opened on her screen. The words *High Tea* were written in an elegant font: gold letters on a china blue background. Coco's initials were monogrammed at the top of the page.

Coco must have hired a Web designer to make this, Haley thought as she clicked on the picture to enter the site.

"You are invited to celebrate the birthday of Coco De Clerq," it said over a photo of the De Clerqs' expansive lawn and white pool-house portico. The place, of course, was fabulous, and Haley knew the party would be too. She tried to imagine herself in this elegant setting, wearing . . . what? Whatever attire was appropriate for this shindig, it wasn't hanging in Haley's closet. If she went to the party, she'd have to take a serious shopping jaunt first.

Haley returned to her in-box and clicked on the next e-mail. It was from Irene Chen and the subject line read, "You might want to get a tattoo after you see this." Inside was a link to the new Web site everyone at school had been constantly mentioning in the halls, Hillsdale Hauntings, along with the coveted password.

Finally! This is it, Haley thought, clicking through to see what all the fuss was about. Under the "Hillsdale Hauntings" banner, a ghost popped up and whispered, "Boo." On a sidebar was a list of videos available for viewing. Haley scanned the choices and clicked on one called "How to Sleep Your Way to a Cover Shoot." She had a feeling she knew who'd be starring in that particular Webisode. And she was right.

The video opened with a shot of Mia Delgado lounging on a mussed-up bed in her underwear—with a guy. She wore a bra and shorts and nothing else, her thick, dark hair sexily messy, a smear of red lipstick on her mouth. She laughed and flirted with the guy, who was lying back and harder to see.

"Want some water?" Mia said in her Spanish accent, taking a glass from the table next to the bed. She playfully poured a little water on the guy in bed with her.

"Hey! Stop it!" he said, but they both just laughed.

"I thought you were thirsty," she said, and splashed a little more on him.

Haley was stunned. Mia Delgado, in her underwear, in bed, for everybody to see! She hadn't expected the videos to be this explicit.

Then Mia fell on top of the guy and started kissing him. Soon they were making out heavily while the video camera rolled. Haley could not believe her eyes. *Who shot this?* she wondered. *And who posted it on this site?*

The video cut off after three minutes, just when things were getting *really* steamy. Haley returned to the menu and scrolled down the page. What else was on this thing? Wait a second . . . what was this video called "Boob Tubing"? She'd heard those words whispered around her a lot lately. She clicked on it, and as soon as the first image flashed on the screen, she had to suppress a shriek of horror.

There she was. Or at least her younger self.

With shaky fingers she clicked Play and the video rolled. It was grainy but beautiful footage, shot with her dad's antique Super 8 camera. There was Haley at age ten in a blue polka-dot bathing suit, riding on an inner tube being pulled at high speed by a motorboat on a lake. Haley remembered this incident with a sense of dread—it was old film from a vacation she'd taken with her family at Lake Tahoe. And she already knew what came next. The inner tube bounced on the waves until it crossed the huge wake of another boat. Haley was dragged through the water and the inner tube went flying. The force of the impact pulled her bathing suit right off her body. And still, the camera rolled.

"Oh no. Oh God no," Haley murmured, shaking her head in disbelief. "I can't be seeing this. This can't be on here! This can't be . . . public!"

The video showed skinny little underdeveloped

Haley washing up on the shore of the lake in her birthday suit. She stumbled onto the beach covering her private parts with her hands and diving for a towel.

The clip finally, mercifully ended. Haley felt faint. Her dad and his stupid camera. She hated it! She'd always hated it. And now look what had happened. She stared at her computer in shock and disbelief.

How could this have happened? Then she remembered her dad's latest project, to transfer all the old Miller home movies onto digital files for easy storage and access. And who, but who had been helping him at the post house? Garrett "the Troll" Noll.

Haley was mortified. She groaned, fell onto the bed, put the pillow over her head and screamed in frustration.

I'll never be able to leave this room again, she thought. *Never ever ever ever ever . . . But even if it's the last thing I do, I will get back at that jerk Garrett for humiliating me like this. Maybe not now, maybe not this year, but someday, and for the rest of his life!*

● ● ●

Poor Haley! She's joined the ranks of Pamela Anderson, Paris Hilton and many more famous faces—and body parts—seen by millions, or in this case hundreds, on the Internet. Sure, she's just a skinny kid in the video, but it's still humiliating. Maybe even more so. This is the kind of

attention Haley could totally live without. One of the worst moments of her young life, replayed over and over for everyone at school to see. Thanks, Dad. Thanks a ton.

Of course, Mia showed almost as much skin as Haley did—and a heck of a lot more curves. Haley couldn't help wondering how Mia felt about her exposure—was she as embarrassed as Haley? Or was she proud of it? Maybe she'd posted the video herself. Haley found that hard to imagine, but anything was possible when it came to Mia Delgado, who was always criticizing Americans for their puritanism.

After those startling home moments, you nearly forgot about Coco's big birthday bash, didn't you? Any party given by the First Girlfriend is bound to be the talk of the town, especially when the governor herself is planning to make an appearance. Haley may feel like hiding in her room forever, but won't she regret missing the party of the year? And won't Coco's blowout eclipse her silly little video anyway?

If you think Haley is experiencing TOTAL MORTIFI-CATION and is never going to leave her bedroom again, turn to page 220. If you think Haley should keep her chin up, face the music and enjoy Coco's birthday party in spite of the haunting video, go to TEA AND SYMPA-THY on page 201. If you are way too curious about that video of Mia and what's behind it, have Haley INVESTI-GATE MIA on page 210. Finally, if you think Haley is feeling so angsty over the leak that she wants to turn to the dark side and punish herself with body art, go with Irene, Shaun and Devon to the TATTOO PARLOR on page 192.

The video is out; the damage has been done. Don't let Haley do anything to make things worse.

PRINCIPAL CRUM'S LITANY

If you think people are whispering behind your back, they probably are.

Haley walked into the auditorium as the students settled in for another rant from Principal Crum, who always seemed to be on the warpath about something. No one took his outrage very seriously, as anyone watching the Hillsdale students (tossing paper airplanes, tweaking each other's hair, tumbling over their seats and laughing and talking as if they were at a house party) could immediately attest.

Principal Crum had just entered the room, so Haley sat down where she was, near the front. She turned around and caught sight of alterna-rebels Devon McKnight, Irene Chen and Shaun Willkommen occupying the nosebleed section with Devon's blond neighbor buddy, Darcy Podowski, by his side. Irene was sketching in a notebook, Shaun was pounding his chest like a gorilla for some unknown reason, and Devon was leaning over and touching Darcy's wrist just where, Haley happened to know, Darcy had a small tattooed blue star. Darcy leaned toward him too, and he held her wrist and lifted it up toward the light to see the tattoo more closely.

Gross, Haley thought, averting her eyes. Why was it so hard to watch Devon with that blond freshman? Haley wasn't sure, but something about the two of them together really bothered her. She looked around the room for something to take her mind off Devon.

The skate crew—Chopper, Troll and associates—crowded into the back corner. Devon hung with them sometimes, but lately he'd been putting more energy into his photography than his shredding. The Troll and Chopper were squirting each other with water guns, only whatever they were shooting wasn't water. Unless water was bright orange, which could happen, Haley thought, if the pollution in New Jersey got bad enough.

The brain trust—Annie Armstrong, Dave Metzger, Hannah Moss and Dale Smithwick—sat near Haley in the front row. Normally Alex Martin might have been with them, since he was cocaptain of the debating team with Annie, but he and Annie were still having shouting matches over his conservative environmental views. Instead, Alex sat near his fellow fiscal conservatives Spencer Eton and Coco De Clerq, although Spencer and Coco did not acknowledge his presence in the least. Coco had a large box in her lap and sat at attention, as if ready to spring something on the masses.

Soccer star and singer-songwriter Sasha Lewis sat in the middle of the room with her boyfriend, Johnny Lane; Cecily Watson; Cecily's guy, Drew Napolitano; and soon-to-be-Sasha's-sister Whitney Klein. Sasha and Whitney appeared to be chummier than ever, now that they were living under the same roof, at least on alternate weekends and three days during the school week. Coco kept stealing annoyed glances at their little clique and then quickly turning away so that they wouldn't know she'd been looking. Not a very effective strategy. Whitney and Sasha continued their whispering and laughing, oblivious, and Haley couldn't help wondering who they were talking about. Coco, perhaps? Or maybe Haley herself?

No sign of Sebastian Bodega or his sexy ex, Mia Delgado, but that didn't strike Haley as strange. She wondered if they had assemblies like this in Spain. She doubted Spanish school principals were as uptight as Principal Crum, but anything was possible.

Principal Crum stormed onto the stage in a huff, dropping papers on the way and bending down to pick them up, which made his pants ride up and showed that he was wearing mismatched socks that day.

"Vermilion Alert, people! Vermilion! A very, very serious matter has come to my attention," he shouted into the microphone. The students quieted down somewhat, but not completely. Principal Crum was not expert at keeping their attention.

"I've just learned of the existence of a Hillsdale High Web site so heinous it defies description. I want you all to know about it so you can keep as far from this filth as possible. The site is called Hillsdale Hauntings."

Bursts of laughter popped up throughout the room. Obviously some people were already well aware of this threat to their mental and moral health. A few people around Haley whispered and she thought some of them were looking at her. *I'm just being paranoid,* she told herself. Why would people be talking about her? She hadn't done anything exceptional lately. She hadn't even had a bad hair day in weeks.

"On this despicable site," Principal Crum said, "someone—a student or students at Hillsdale, as I understand it—has posted explicit video footage of some of our own students. These videos contain graphic language and even some brief nudity—"

Now the room really buzzed, and again Haley got the feeling, stronger this time, that people were pointing and whispering about her.

"I want you all to avoid it like the plague! Someone is violating the privacy of our students. It's illegal and immoral, and I will get to the bottom of it."

On the word "bottom," Shaun Willkommen stood up and slapped his butt.

Great, Haley thought. Principal Crum doesn't want people to see the site? Then why did he just advertise it to the whole school? No one could resist logging on to Hillsdale Hauntings now.

"I'd like to get to the bottoms of some of it too," a guy yelled out from the back.

"Who said that?" Principal Crum's face was red with rage. Haley wondered if he used the color of his face to determine what kind of alert he called when trouble arose. If today was a Vermilion Alert, the principal's skin tone certainly matched it. "Who said that? Never mind. I'll find you. I'll find the perpetrators of this terrible crime against our modesty and good taste. And when I do it will be no joking matter, I promise you that. Now, since this is an Internet problem, we need to fight technical expertise with technical expertise. Not my forte, so I'd like to enlist the help of our school's finest scientific minds. Where are Hannah Moss and Dave Metzger?"

Hannah and Dave raised their hands.

"Right here in the front row, I see," Principal

Crum said. "Good. You two will be in charge of tracking down the culprit behind this perverted Web site. If anyone knows anything about this case, I demand that you turn the offender in to school authorities at once! Is that clear?"

From the back someone shouted, "Watch out for that killer wave!" Heads turned toward Haley. *Why?* she wondered.

There were giggles throughout the crowd. Haley was baffled. What was this all about? And why did it sound vaguely, creepily familiar?

"All right, people," Principal Crum said. "That is all for now. I expect you to help us catch the criminal in our midst and stop the spread of Internet perversion now! You are dismissed."

As the assembly broke up, Haley heard people making fun of Principal Crum and echoing the lines she'd just heard about the killer wave and "towel, please." She felt uncomfortable. She tried to tell herself that everyone had days like this, that nothing was really wrong, but she couldn't quite convince herself.

Coco threaded her way through the crowd, using this opportunity to pass out invitations to her exclusive birthday party. It was going to be big, but not that big—plenty of people at school weren't invited, and Coco made sure they knew it. To those who were invited, however, she couldn't have been more gracious.

"Here you are, Zach," Coco said, giving Zach Woolsey, a senior soccer player, one of her fancy robin's-egg-blue envelopes. "I hope you can make it. The governor will be there."

As she passed Haley, she paused, and Haley expected to receive an envelope. Instead Coco said, under her breath, "Yours is in the mail." Then she breezed past Haley, leaving a trail of French perfume in her wake.

● ● ●

"Yours is in the mail"? What was that all about? Was Coco too embarrassed to be seen in public inviting Haley to her party? Did she invite Haley at all?

Or maybe Haley's just having a paranoid day. Why is she feeling so insecure all of a sudden? Is it just her imagination, or is there a reason for it? Principal Crum himself said that salacious videos of some students have been posted online—could that lead Haley to the answers she's looking for? If you think Haley needs to find out immediately just what's on that Hillsdale Hauntings Web site, send her home on page 220 (TOTAL MORTIFICATION).

Or maybe you think Haley's just having an off day, and by tomorrow everything will be back to normal and Coco's party invitation will show up in the mail. If you think she can't wait to witness the most decadent bash of the year, turn to page 201, TEA AND SYMPATHY.

In other news, why do Devon's attentions to Darcy

bother Haley so much? Do you think he really goes for freshman meat, or is he just being neighborly to the budding blonde? Or maybe he's just way into tattoos all of a sudden. It's possible. To hang with the alternative clique and find out just how into tattoos Devon really is these days, go to the TATTOO PARLOR on page 192.

Principal Crum is right about one thing: something creepy is going on at Hillsdale. Haley sees trouble everywhere she looks. But she can't be everywhere at once. At some point she has to choose a direction. Correction: You have to choose one for her.

LADY-IN-WAITING

**The best way to make
a queen bee sting is
to give her the wrong
kind of flowers.**

"Oh, look at this," Coco said, nearly spitting in disgust. She had brought Haley along on her birthday party prep errands and the first stop was Hillsdale Stationers, where she'd planned to pick up her invitations.

Haley picked up one of Coco's birthday invitations and examined the heavy cream-colored stock and glimmering gold lettering.

"It looks beautiful to me," she said.

"Are you blind?" Coco snapped. "It's wrong. All

wrong!" She threw one of the cards at the woman behind the counter. "I specifically requested these invitations be engraved, not letter-pressed! How do you expect me to send these out with the governor's name on them? They're a disgrace!"

"But you said you needed the invitations in a week," the stationer said. "And there's no way engraved invitations could be ready that fast—"

"No way? You *find* a way," Coco said.

"Coco, I really don't see how anyone could ever tell the difference," Haley said. She'd never even heard about letterpress versus engraving, and she seriously doubted that anyone at Hillsdale High besides Coco De Clerq had heard of it either.

"It's very easy," Coco said, turning one of the cards over. "Feel that." She rubbed Haley's fingers over the smooth back of the card. "See! Any idiot can tell in two seconds that the card has not been engraved."

"Sorry," Haley said. "But I still don't think—"

"How can you give me letterpress for the money I'm paying you?" Coco said to the store owner, interrupting Haley. "I gave you a week's notice. That should be plenty of time. Find a way to make this happen or I'll take my business elsewhere. And you don't want that—our new governor will be throwing a lot of parties."

"I'm terribly sorry, Miss De Clerq," the woman said. "We'll correct the error at once."

"See that you do." Coco stormed out of the shop, Haley at her heels. "I can't believe that place. You'd think a girl like me could get decent service in this hick town, but no. . . ."

They walked down the block and turned into Frilly Lily, the best florist in town. A silver bell jingled as they waltzed in. The room was tastefully abloom with exotic flowers and creative, unusual arrangements. This was no ordinary flower shop. Haley was instantly impressed.

"Yes, may I help you?" The young man behind the counter had a thin mustache and glasses.

"My name is Coco De Clerq, and I'm here to see the sample centerpieces Josette has made up for me. I hope they're ready."

"Certainly, Miss De Clerq," the young man said. "I'll be right back."

A minute later he reappeared with a towering arrangement of white calla lilies, forget-me-nots and exotic vines in a tall glass vase. "Here we are. I think we'll be pleased."

"Ugh, are you kidding?" Coco cried. "We're not pleased—not pleased at all! What is Josette thinking? The governor will be at this party. The governor! And my theme is English rose. Calla lilies are deco blooms, and therefore not romantic enough. I want every single flower to feel as if it has just been plucked from a garden in Sussex—"

"But Miss De Clerq, it's December," the clerk

said. "We have trouble finding choice flowers in bloom at this time of year. The shipping process tends to—"

"Totally beside the point!" Coco shouted. "The room should be dripping with fragrance and color. Any moron could figure this out. And how dare you show me a plain glass vase? This is just for the sample, I hope."

"Actually, we thought the simplicity looked nice with—"

"Simplicity is for simpletons!" Haley flinched at Coco's harsh tone. "Anyone can put flowers in a glass vase, for heaven's sake. Why would I pay for that? I specifically told Josette I wanted something rich and lush." She grabbed a catalog sitting on the counter and quickly flipped through it. "There." She stabbed a photo with her finger. It showed an array of vintage china vases, very expensive-looking. "I want these."

"But these have to be special-ordered," the clerk said. "It could take weeks—"

"Get them here in time," Coco said. "Find a way. This is exactly what I want—and it's a much more proper height for a table centerpiece than this tall cylinder."

"All right, I'll see what I can do."

"Good," Coco said. "Tell Josette to call me when she's reworked the flowers to a civilized standard."

The young man was practically shaking. Haley felt sorry for him. Coco was certainly turning into a tyrant over these party details. Not that she'd ever been easy to deal with.

They flounced out of the florist shop. "Whew. I need a cappy," Coco said. "We've earned it. Who knew event planning could be so strenuous? I feel like I've just gotten a workout."

"Yeah, way to work up a sweat," Haley teased.

"We do deserve a break," Coco exclaimed. They wandered the block to Drip coffeehouse and settled at a cozy table for cappuccinos. "This party is going to be the death of me," Coco said.

If you don't kill some poor florist first, Haley thought, but she didn't dare say it. She didn't need to bring the wrath of Coco down on her own head. That was one guillotine she was desperate to avoid.

"So, everybody is talking about that skank Mia Delgado," Coco said. "Have you heard what they're saying now? Supposedly there's this new Web site with sexy videos of girls from our school on it. I heard one of the perviest clips shows Mia hooking up with some older guy. Ew. Can you imagine?"

"Uh, I try not to," Haley said. She'd heard rumors about this site too, but she'd brushed them off, figuring it was probably just normal boy talk—in other words, exaggeration.

"I wonder who the guy is," Coco said, topping her cappuccino with cinnamon. "Probably Whitney's dad. Would that not be the grossest?"

"Yuck," Haley said. Whitney Klein's dad, Jerry, had been caught flirting with the leggy Spanish model more than once, so it wasn't impossible. Still, Haley shuddered at the thought.

"At least his breath is probably minty fresh," Coco said. Jerry, who was known as the breath spray king of New Jersey, had made his money manufacturing pocket-sized spritzers.

Coco's expression suddenly changed from grossed-out to seriously concerned. "I've heard there are videos up of other girls we know, too. Supposedly, there's a video of . . . you, Haley."

Haley almost dropped her coffee in her lap. "Me? How could there be a video of me?"

Then Haley remembered that her dad was currently transferring all the old Miller home movies to digital format at a local post house—where Garrett "the Troll" Noll just happened to work. Suddenly, Haley herself was concerned.

Coco shrugged. "That's what I heard. I haven't seen it yet. . . ."

Haley tried to remember if she had done anything particularly embarrassing while her dad was filming. It wasn't an impossible task, since her dad was almost always filming, and Haley was, well, accident-prone.

"I keep meaning to check out the site, but I've been so busy with the party," Coco said. "Spencer did say he saw you. Not that he's the most reliable source on the planet, but on the other hand, why would he lie about something like that?"

Haley felt her stomach flip. "What else did he say?"

"I wasn't really listening," Coco replied, as Haley gritted her teeth in frustration. "But he did mention something about an inner tube. Whatever that means. Sounds kinky. Guess you're not quite as *innocent* as we all thought."

Haley practically shrieked. That was it, the video that was now floating around the Internet for all the world to see. Her most embarrassing moment ever, captured on a family vacation to Lake Tahoe. Haley had been riding an inner tube pulled by a speedboat—until she and the boat hit a wake. The force of the impact stripped off her bathing suit, so her underdeveloped ten-year-old body had been bared for all the world—and her father's Super 8 camera—to see. Perry had thought it was cute and funny, in a Lucille Ball sort of way, but Haley still thought of it as one of the worst moments of her life, especially since a cute sixteen-year-old lifeguard named Trevor could be seen chuckling along with her dad on the tape.

• • •

Poor Haley. This certainly isn't the first time she's felt like going into hiding. But this time, will she be able to live down the infamy? How will she face everyone back at school now that she knows they've all seen her younger self naked?

Coco can certainly be a dictator when it comes to party planning. Yikes. Anyone who works for her needs a seriously thick skin. Coco is convinced that brow-beating everyone in sight is the best way to get things done, and who knows, maybe she's right. Her current birthday party stands to top last year's. She's certainly focusing on every tiny detail with microscopic precision. But will Hillsdale's racy new Web site eclipse even the party of the year? It seems pretty certain that Mia will be the talk of the town for the days, weeks and even months to come—and that wouldn't be out of character.

If you're sure that the mere thought of such an embarrassing moment being posted online will send Haley running home immediately to hide in her bedroom and never come out, turn to page 220 (TOTAL MORTIFI-CATION). If you think Haley can handle whatever comes her way and is not about to let a little video footage keep her from Coco's party turn to page 201, TEA AND SYMPATHY.

Who's the mystery guy in the video with Mia? Haley doesn't know, but if it is Whitney's father, the damage will be widespread and massive. If you think Haley should find out if there's any truth to Coco's speculation about Mia and Jerry Klein, New Jersey's breath spray king, join forces with Whitney and Sasha on page 215, GETTING FRESH. Finally, if you think Haley should IN-VESTIGATE MIA before she jumps to any conclusions, turn to page 210.

BOOB TUBING

Ordering pizza can be dangerous, and not just because of the calories.

"I'm thinking hoop skirts and corsets," Whitney Klein said as she put the finishing touches on a coat of coral toenail polish. "Updated, of course. Shorter, a full skirt, nipped waist, something silky . . ."

Sasha, who was going for a funkier navy polish on her toes, said, "I'm not sure I want to go along with Coco's whole English rose theme. I mean, I know she's the First Girlfriend now, but does that mean we all have to go proper and have tea with her under the heaters on her lawn?"

Haley and Sasha were hanging out at Whitney Klein's dad's house, talking about what to wear to Coco's upcoming birthday bash at the De Clerq manse. Haley's invitation had just arrived in the mail that very morning.

"I think she just wants everyone to look elegant," Haley said, surveying her pearly pink toes. "And more interesting than their everyday school selves. The invitation was pretty, wasn't it?"

"I love the gold lettering," Whitney said. "I just love gold in general. Color something gold and you've pretty much got me."

"Maybe I'll wear a gold dress," Sasha said. "Long and lean like a glass of champagne. If only I could find one."

"I could make you a dress like that," Whitney offered. She'd started her own clothing line, WK, which had already had some success in the trendier local boutiques. "If I have enough time before the party."

"That would be amazing," Sasha said. "Thanks, Whit. What about you, Haley? What are you going to wear to the Cocothon?"

"I don't know," Haley said. "I want something sophisticated, but I'm afraid I can't pull it off."

"That's ridiculous," Whitney said. "You put on a sophisticated dress, you become sophisticated. Simple as that."

"I'm not so sure," Haley said. "I've tried on fancy

dresses before and just felt like a little girl swimming in her mother's clothes."

Whitney stood up to survey Haley's figure, careful not to smudge her toenail polish. "Hmm . . . You know what would look great on you? A cashmere sweater with a poufy skirt. Classic and simple. And maybe a jeweled headband for sparkle . . ."

"That's too casual for this party," Sasha said. "I think you should go nuts, Haley. Bugle beads, sequins, slinky satin, the whole shebang."

"But that's completely out of character for me," Haley said.

"Exactly!" Sasha said. "Live a little, Miller. How many chances do you get in this boring town to really dress up? Might as well go for it."

"Is anybody else hungry?" Whitney said. "Talking about clothes always makes me hungry."

"Talking about anything makes you hungry," Sasha said.

"I could eat something," Haley said.

"I'll order a pizza," Whitney said. "What's the number for Lisa's?"

"I don't know," Sasha said. "I thought you'd have it memorized."

"Very funny," Whitney said. "I think Dad's got it on his computer." She hurried into her father's office. Whitney's dad, Jerry Klein, owned a company that manufactured breath spray, among other things, and sometimes worked from home.

"Does talking about clothes make *you* hungry?" Haley asked.

"No," Sasha said. "Talking about boys makes me hungry."

"Oh my God!" Whitney gasped from the other room. "I don't believe this!"

Haley and Sasha ran into Mr. Klein's office. It was neat and spare, with a new computer on the desk. Whitney was staring at the screen in shock.

"I logged on to get the pizza number," Whitney said. "And found that Dad has bookmarked Hillsdale Hauntings!"

"That site everybody's been talking about?" Haley asked.

"With all the Girls Gone Wild videos of kids at school . . . ," Sasha said.

"Why would he be looking at this?" Whitney said. "Isn't that kind of . . ." She couldn't finish the thought, so Haley finished it for her.

"Creepy?" Haley said.

Whitney clicked on a video. "Here's the last posting he watched. Oh my God—not her again."

A grainy video played. Haley gasped when she saw who was starring in it: none other than Mia Delgado. She was lying in bed with some guy, wearing nothing but a bra and shorts, rolling around and making out with him.

"Oh my . . . ," Sasha said.

"Gross," Haley added.

"Yet somehow I can't stop watching," Sasha replied.

"Why is he watching this?" Whitney cried. "Why is my father watching videos of teenaged girls? Why is my father such a disgusting jerk? Isn't Trish enough for him?"

"Maybe he was trying to protect you," Haley said. "Maybe he heard about the site and wanted to make sure you weren't on it."

"Sure," Sasha said. "That's probably all it was."

"Maybe . . . ," Whitney said, but nobody believed it. Jerry Klein had been seen flirting with Mia before, and some people said he'd done more than that, even though Mia was only his daughter's age. Haley felt sorry for Whitney, and sorry for Mia, too, being exposed in this humiliating way.

"Let's see who else is on here," Sasha announced, hoping to change the subject and scrolling down the list of contents. She clicked on a video. Up popped an image of a young girl in a bathing suit—an uncannily familiar young girl.

"Haley—isn't that . . . you?" Sasha asked.

Haley felt a pit forming in her stomach. It was her, all right. She was ten years old, on vacation with her family at Lake Tahoe, riding on an inner tube being pulled by a motorboat. She was laughing and having a great time—but Haley knew what was coming next.

"Oh God," she groaned. "How did this get on here?"

"What?" Whitney asked. "It doesn't seem so bad to me. You're so cute. Flat, but cute."

Haley swallowed. *Just wait*, she thought. And then it happened.

The inner tube crossed the wake of another boat— a much bigger boat. Haley hit a huge wave, tumbled off the inner tube and lost her bathing suit in the process. She washed ashore totally naked, covering her private parts with her hands and screaming.

Good old Dad and his ever-present video camera.

Whitney said nothing, but Sasha burst out laughing. "That is hysterical! You were adorable!"

"I wasn't adorable, I was naked," Haley said, stone-faced. "It isn't funny. The whole world can now see me naked! This is a nightmare!"

"Come on, Haley, it's not that bad," Sasha said. "This video was shot ages ago. It's ancient history. It's not as if you look like that anymore." She nodded at the image of skinny ten-year-old Haley on the screen, versus the more voluptuous version standing in front of her. "You were a baby then. You're all grown up now."

"You don't get it," Haley said. She couldn't believe this was happening to her. It was one thing for Mia to be caught hooking up on the Internet—that was shocking, yet somehow less than surprising. But

Haley was different. She actually valued her privacy—and her modesty. And now the whole school, maybe the whole town, had seen her naked. It made her want to puke.

She looked at Whitney, who was staring at the floor, her face ashen white. Haley exchanged a glance with Sasha, and knew they were thinking the same thing: Whitney was still fixated on her dad and the dirty Mia videos.

"Whit?" Sasha said. "Are you okay?"

"He's obsessed with her," Whitney said quietly. "He's obsessed with Mia, a girl my age. It's twisted."

"Whitney, listen. . . ." Haley didn't know what to say next, so she blurted out, "What about that pizza?"

"I'm going to find him. I'm going to track him down at work," Whitney said, shaking off Sasha's comforting arm. "I'm going to let him know exactly what I think of him. And he'll be sorry."

"I'll drive," Sasha said collecting her thoughts. "Sisters to the end."

● ● ●

Whoa. Major scandals going down left and right. This Hillsdale Hauntings site is exposing people like crazy—and not just the girls on the videos, but the people who watch them, too. Whitney may have thought that whole mess between her father and Mia had blown over, but apparently she was wrong. She's caught him watching a rather graphic video of the Spanish beauty and has jumped to the conclusion that he is somehow obsessed with her—entirely inappropriately, of course.

Jerry Klein has embarrassed his daughter long enough, no question about it. If you think confronting the breath spray king at his headquarters in the middle of the workday is the right thing to do, send Haley off with Whitney and Sasha to page 215, GETTING FRESH.

Meanwhile, Mia's raw footage leaves several questions unanswered, such as who posted it on the Internet? And who was that guy she was hooking up with? If you think Haley is curious about the behind-the-scenes story of the Mia makeout show, turn to page 210, INVESTIGATE MIA.

But don't forget, Haley's a victim of this Internet outrage herself. If you think the shame over her naked video footage is too much for Haley to bare—er, bear—have her hole up in her bedroom and hide from public life forever on page 220, TOTAL MORTIFICATION.

Finally, if you think no video leak is going to stop Haley from being present for Coco's birthday extravaganza, turn to page 201, TEA AND SYMPATHY.

People respond to adversity in a variety of ways. The path they choose can determine their future. Don't ruin Haley's; choose wisely and well.

HOOP DREAMS

You can't always trust the motives of someone who plays the hero.

"**C**ome on, come on . . . ," Haley chanted as Spencer Eton grabbed the ball from a Westwood player and took a shot from the three-point line—his fourth three-point attempt of the game. "Make it, make it!"

The ball bounced off the rim and a Westwood player caught it on the rebound and ran with it down the court.

"Oh . . . ," Haley groaned, along with the rest of the Hillsdale crowd.

"Why does Spencer keep doing that?" Whitney

said. "Doesn't he get it yet? When he shoots from far away like that he's going to miss!"

"He's a showboater," Sasha said. "And he's blowing the game."

Haley sighed as Westwood scored again, closing in on Hillsdale 35–37. She was sitting in the gym bleachers with Sasha and Whitney for Hillsdale's first real match-up of the season, and the first game with the injured Reese Highland sitting on the sidelines. Spencer had volunteered to replace Reese, and everyone had cheered him on. Now that was looking like a shaky idea. Not that Spencer wasn't talented— he just didn't know how to play with a team.

Spencer caught the ball on Westwood's rim and dribbled down the court. "Pass! Pass to Johnny!" Sasha shouted, but Spencer didn't listen. Instead he went for a fancy spinning layup and bounced the ball off the backboard. Missed again.

"You suck, Eton!" Sasha shouted.

"Sasha, he's still on our team," Haley reminded her.

"I know, but he's really pissing me off," Sasha screamed over boos from the stands. "He won't give up the ball." Her boyfriend, Johnny Lane, played defense but was also one of the Hawks' high scorers. "We usually beat Westwood easily, and look, they're two points away from tying up the game."

The ref blew his whistle and called time out. The Hillsdale cheerleaders, led by Cecily Watson, rushed onto the court for a quick morale boost. "Here we go, blue and gold, here we go!" The crowd clap-clapped along with them. The game resumed.

Drew Napolitano passed to Spencer, then dashed to an open spot and held out his hands for the ball. This was obviously a play they'd practiced with the coach, but Spencer didn't seem to see that both Drew and Johnny were wide open as he once again drove right into a Westwood trap and lost the ball. Johnny scowled and snarled something in frustration to Drew.

"This is driving Johnny crazy, I know it," Sasha said. "Spencer is just not a team player."

Haley had to admit that this sad observation looked truer with every play. Johnny, a much more reliable shooter than Spencer, was wide open for the next three possessions, but Spencer refused to feed him the ball down low, even when Johnny was positioned for an easy shot. The Hawks' defense kept Westwood from scoring, but they needed to move ahead by a few more points or a foul could lose them the game.

"Where's Coco?" Whitney asked, losing interest in the game and scanning the crowd instead. "It's not like her to miss a big event like this—her darling Spencer's very first showing on the basketball court."

"Maybe she can't stand the sight of ball-hogging," Sasha said. "I know I can't."

"Did you get your invitation to her party yet?" Haley asked. Hers had arrived that day in the mail. "It's fancier than most wedding invitations I've seen."

"Totally," Sasha said. "All that gold lettering . . ."

"I loved it," Whitney said. "That thick creamy paper stock . . . It was beautiful. I can't wait to go to the party. Say what you like about Coco, she knows how to spend money and do it up right."

Sasha laughed. "Like spending money is such a great talent to have. Who doesn't know how to spend money?"

"But there's an art to it," Whitney protested. "That's why—"

She froze, her eyes fixed on the lower bleachers. Haley looked down and saw Mia Delgado walking into the gym and looking for a place to sit down. Whitney bristled and dug her nails into Haley's arm.

"I can't believe she has the nerve to show her face here," Whitney said. "I could just scratch her eyes out."

"Whitney, ow," Haley said. "You're scratching me up instead."

"Sorry." Whitney let go of Haley's arm. "She's just so disgusting I can hardly stand it!"

"What did she do now?" Haley asked.

"You haven't heard about the infamous video?" Sasha said.

Haley had heard rumors swirling around school

about a Web site with skin-heavy videos of Hillsdale girls, but she'd assumed this was all the product of some oversexed sophomore boy's imagination. Apparently she was wrong.

"My dad has the clip of Mia on his computer," Whitney whispered. "I saw it when I was in his office the other day. He had it bookmarked! Just thinking about it makes me crazy. It's so gross! Why would he want to look at her like that?"

"Why would anyone," Sasha sighed.

"What's in the clip?" Haley asked innocently.

"It shows Mia hooking up with some guy," Whitney said. "She's half naked and rolling around on some silk-sheeted bed—"

"And who's the guy?" Haley asked.

"I don't know and I don't care," Whitney said. "I just wish Mia would stay away from my father."

Whitney's dad ought to stay away from Mia was more like it, Haley though, but she of course couldn't say that to sensitive Whitney. "Have you said anything to him about it?"

"Not yet," Whitney replied. "But I'd like to tell him how pissed off I am about it. I can't stop thinking about it. It's ruining my life!"

"Maybe he has some kind of explanation," Haley said.

"Maybe," Whitney said, but behind her back Sasha shook her head no. "Like what?"

"You should really check out the site," Sasha added

to Haley. "It's called Hillsdale Hauntings. I mean, you might want to see what *else* is posted on there."

"What are you talking about?" Haley looked at Sasha, who clamped her mouth shut with a guilty "I don't want to be the one to break it to you" expression on her face. Whitney, however, had no problem with being the one to divulge bad news to anyone.

"There's a video of you on there, Haley," Whitney announced. "It's called 'Boob Tubing' and it's getting tons of hits."

"Of me?" Haley was horrified. "What's 'Boob Tubing'? What does it show?"

"It's hard to explain," Whitney said. "Just see for yourself."

"Sasha?" Haley turned to her more sensible friend for help, but Sasha just shrugged.

"It's really something you should see for yourself," Sasha agreed. "It kind of defies description."

"Oh my God. . . ." Haley suddenly had a terrible headache. What kind of video footage of her could there possibly be?

No one would answer her questions. The look on Sasha's face told her that whatever was up online was something she needed to see, pronto.

● ● ●

This Hillsdale Hauntings Web site is really rocking the school, tearing up lives, threatening family ties . . . Whitney is certainly upset about her father's Mia Delgado obsession, and it's hard to blame her. It's just so . . . icky. Still, it's possible Whitney is exaggerating the seediness of the situation—she's not exactly what's known as a reliable source. If Haley wants to find out the honest truth, she may have to look into the story herself.

But Haley's got her own problems to deal with first. What exactly can people see of her on this "Boob Tubing" video? Provocative title. Just what Haley needs. You have to admit this doesn't sound good for her.

If you think Haley should go home right away and see what's posted online, turn to page 220, TOTAL MORTIFICATION. If you want to join Whitney and Sasha as they storm into Whitney's dad's office to confront him about Mia Delgado, turn to page 215, GETTING FRESH. If you think Haley wants to INVESTIGATE MIA first, go to page 210 to find out more about Mia's checkered past than you might have wanted to know.

BUMP AND GRIND

No one is good
at everything,
not even geniuses.

"Hey, Annie! Happy birthday!"

Haley waved across the DMV parking lot at Annie Armstrong, who was just getting into the driver's test car with an official from the Department of Motor Vehicles. Annie grinned and waved back like an astronaut preparing to blast into space. Haley had decided to go with Dave Metzger and Alex Martin to surprise Annie at the DMV. It was Annie's seventeenth birthday and she was eager to get her driver's license. From what Haley had seen of Annie's driver's-ed practice, though, Annie could use all the support she could get.

"I hope she passes," Dave said nervously. Since he always seemed at least a little on edge, it was hard to tell if he was really worried that Annie wouldn't pass her test, or just his usual baseline jittery self. Haley knew Dave had seen Annie's student driving too, so she had to figure he was just as afraid Annie would screw something up. To take his mind off it, he pulled out his ever-present handheld computer and started searching, for further information on his long-lost dad, no doubt.

Annie started the test car, with the official—a chubby middle-aged man with the thick steel-gray hair of a former Soviet party leader—riding shotgun. She drove down the test course, weaving unsteadily through a maze of orange traffic cones. Haley bit her lip as Annie nearly hit the first cone, then the second, but swerved away each time at the last possible minute.

"Have you ever been to Storm King?" Alex asked Haley as they watched Annie's tentative maneuvers. Haley shook her head. "It's a sculpture garden in upstate New York. Huge fields with gigantic sculptures by famous artists like Henry Moore and Alexander Calder."

"I love Calder's mobiles," Haley said, now half interested.

"They've got some of those there," Alex said.

"Listen, I was thinking of driving up there next weekend, if you felt like coming along—"

"Storm King? Upstate New York, did you say?" Dave's ears perked up, but his eyes were still glued to his computer, where he had apparently searched for and found a Web site for the sculpture garden. "Mountainville, New York. That's not far from Newburgh."

Alex looked a little annoyed at the interruption. "So?"

"So? Didn't I tell you?" Dave seemed very excited now. He'd forgotten to watch Annie, who was performing left and right turns for the DMV guy. "I found my father! I finally actually tracked him down. He lives in Newburgh, which, according to this map, is not at all far from Storm King." On his computer screen, which he now showed to Haley and Alex, was a driving map with directions from Mountainville to Newburgh highlighted. They were indeed quite near each other.

"That's great, Dave," Haley said, trying to be supportive.

"Yeah, great," Alex said warily, as if he knew what might be coming next. And boy was he right.

"I was thinking, my mother will never in a million years give me permission to see him," Dave began tentatively. "Especially now that she's bonkers over Rick Von Time Trap. But she would let me go to a sculpture garden—and the Rickster would be all over that. Me seeing art and everything—he's always trying to get me to go to museums and stuff. Even if my mother didn't like the idea of me going away on my own without her and everything, Rick could talk her into it." He looked up at Haley and Alex, clearly expecting to now be met with an invitation to join them on their trip. Haley could tell that Alex had never meant to include Dave—much less Annie—on their little excursion.

"Uh, Dave, see, the thing is . . ." Alex hemmed and hawed but seemed to have trouble finding the words to tell Dave to buzz off. Haley had never seen Alex at a loss for words before.

"Hey, look," Haley said, hoping to ease the tension by changing the subject. "Annie's doing great so far. She's actually backing up—"

Oh no—Annie was backing up. This was her weakest driving skill, and the others weren't exactly well honed. Haley cringed as Annie hit the gas, heading right for a parked car. She tried and failed to slow down before she bumped into the other automobile and ground up against it until its bumper cracked off.

"Ooh, that's not good," Alex said, shaking his head.

"Poor Annie," Haley said.

"She probably should have practiced more before taking the test," Dave said.

The DMV guy got out of the car, his face red, and

stared in disbelief at the damage done. He gave Annie a pink slip and sent her packing. Choking back tears, she ran across the parking lot to the sidelines, where her friends were waiting for her.

"I don't believe it!" she cried. "I failed!"

"What happened out there?" Alex asked.

"I tried to brake, but I kept stepping on the gas by mistake," Annie said. "What a disaster. I can't believe I gave up Coco's party for this."

"Rookie mistake," Haley said. "Anyone could have done it." She'd brought a novelty birthday horn to toot in celebration after Annie's test but thought maybe now wasn't the time.

"I've never failed a test before in my life," Annie said, tearing up. "This is the worst birthday ever."

Dave put his arms around her and tried to console her. "It's just a driving test, sweetie. Any moron can pass it."

Annie started crying harder. Haley glared at Dave. She knew he meant well but he could be so clueless sometimes.

"What Dave meant to say is that it's not a big deal," Haley said. "You can retake the test in a few weeks. You're sure to pass it next time." She glanced past the sobbing Annie at Alex, who shrugged as if to say *I wouldn't be so sure.*

"Do you really think so?" Annie said.

"Of course we do," Haley said. Just then she felt her phone vibrate. She turned away from the group and reached into her pocket for a quick glance at the screen. It was a text message from Matt Graham, one of Spencer Eton's friends from the last boarding school he'd been kicked out of.

"SIGMA @ Eton's," the message said, and gave her a password to get in. "Just like old times."

Hmmm, Haley thought. Matt Graham? She hadn't heard from him in a long time. What made him think of her all of a sudden? SIGMA, Spencer Eton's exclusive club, was known as the place to go if you were looking for a good time. Anything could happen at a SIGMA party, and anything usually did.

Haley tried not to show her reaction to the message so that Alex wouldn't wonder who'd just texted her and ask. She knew Alex didn't think much of Spencer and his crew—and he might not think much of Haley if he knew she'd be willing to hang out with them.

"Guess what? This will cheer you up!" Dave said to Annie, giving her a squeeze. "We're going on a road trip with Alex and Haley. We're going upstate to see my dad."

"Really?" This news did seem to lift Annie's spirits. "That's great! When?"

"Well, we haven't actually settled anything yet," Alex said, giving Haley a "Get me out of this" look. Haley shrugged. What could she do? Annie was her friend, and so was Dave. Wasn't she obligated to help them both out?

· · ·

It's been a while since we've heard about SIGMA—Mrs. Eton's political ambitions may have put a lid on Spencer's wild partying for a time, but it's back, baby, and Haley knows the crème de la crème of Hillsdale teen society is going to be there. The question is, does she care? Why did Matt Graham invite her? Is he interested in her, or does he have an ulterior motive? There's only one way to find out—by going to the party.

Or does Haley care more about the bookishly cute and very smart Alex Martin? He just asked her to take a road trip with him—that's a pretty serious date. Of course, with Dave and Annie tagging along, it might not end up being particularly romantic. Haley will have to take her chances.

If you think Haley should go with Alex on the road trip to STORM KING, even if Dave and Annie are along for the ride, turn to page 226. If you think Haley is more curious about Matt's out-of-the-blue invitation to SIGMA, go to page 242, OLD HABITS.

Haley may be able to fit in with all different kinds of people, from the most bookish to the most rebellious to the snootiest, but there comes a time when you have to choose your friends and stick by them.

TATTOO PARLOR

Before you tattoo a name on your heart, be sure it's true love.

"**T**his is the place," Darcy said. She'd led Haley, Devon, Shaun and Irene to Tommy's Tattoos, the spot that had given her the little star on her wrist. Tommy's was a dingy storefront in the Floods with a hand-painted psychedelic sign. Everyone followed Darcy inside, clutching the designs they'd drawn in art class. Haley had even brought along her pathetic butterfly drawing, to prove to the others that she was just as serious about getting a tattoo as they were—even though she wasn't sure she'd really go through with it. It was just that everyone, especially Devon, seemed to think Darcy's tat was so cool, and Haley couldn't help feeling that she had to try to keep up with Blondie, even if the girl was only a freshman. Something about the way Devon looked at her rattled Haley.

Inside, a tattoo needle buzzed over the sound of blaring hip-hop music. A girl with stringy blue hair greeted them at a desk. Tattoos covered every inch of her arms like colorful vines. "You all getting tats today?" she asked.

"Yep, all of us," Shaun said. "Me first."

"Cool," the girl said. "Go see Viper." She pointed to a booth manned by a bald guy in a leather vest with no shirt underneath—the better to show off the blue mermaid on his chest. "You can all go watch if you want. It'll be a while before we can fit the rest of you in."

Shaun sat down at Viper's table while the others gathered around. "What can I do you for?" Viper asked. "Is this your first?"

"Yes, sir. I am a tattoo virgin, but I promise I will be back for more." Shaun pulled out the tiger he had drawn, stared at it and shook his head. "I wanted to get this on my butt, but then I changed my mind."

"You're chickening out already?" Darcy asked.

"No, I just want a different picture for my first

tattoo. It's got to mean something." He waved at Irene to hand over her octopus doodle. "Rini, do you mind if I brand your octopus on my forearm?"

Irene grinned. "I'd be honored." She gave her drawing to Viper to copy. Viper nodded appreciatively. "Nice work. Okay, kid, let's do this thing."

He started tracing lines on Shaun's arm, outlining the future tattoo. Irene homed in, watching carefully, as if she was worried that Viper might somehow screw up her drawing. "Don't make the tentacles too short," she warned.

"I got it, honey," Viper said, sternly. "I've been tattooing skin for a long time. I know what I'm doing. Now, this may hurt a little. . . ."

Irene squinted at him. She wasn't about to take his word for it. She had to keep an eye on him or Shaun could be scarred forever by poorly drawn body art.

"Check this wall of unicorns," Darcy said to Devon, pointing at a panel tacked to the drywall that formed Viper's booth. At least a dozen varieties of unicorns lined up among the stars, dragons, anchors, pinups and other suggested tattoo designs. Pink ones, white ones, unicorns with flowers on their heads, with barefoot princesses riding on them, with angel's wings, ridden by cats . . .

Devon laughed. "I had no idea unicorns could have pierced tongues."

Darcy laughed too, conspiratorially, and turned away from Haley as if to leave her out of the conversation.

"I know, right? I hate unicorns. They're so lame. And I hate the kind of girl who loves unicorns, you know what I mean? They're like the horsey type, only a hundred times worse."

"I call them fairy children," Devon said. "There was a whole clique of them at art school. Big users of glitter gel pens."

"And dotting their *is* with hearts," Haley said, trying to find a way in. "Or stars. And putting sparkles on everything . . ."

Darcy and Devon just stared at her as if she'd said the dumbest thing they'd ever heard. But why was what she'd said any stupider than their dopey unicorn comments?

"So what kind of tattoo do you think I should get next?" Darcy asked, very pointedly to Devon and only Devon.

How about a witch? Haley thought. *Or a tiny, tiny, annoying little mosquito, right where your brain is supposed to be?*

"I don't know," Devon said. "Do you want a little one, like your star?" He picked up her wrist to look at the star again. He seemed to take every opportunity to touch her tattoo. "Or a big one, like a dragon or something?"

"I think I'll stick with small and subtle for now," Darcy said. "It's sexier, don't you think?"

Devon nodded. "How about a half-moon, to go with the star?"

Haley yawned. Irene and Shaun were completely caught up in watching Viper work, and Devon and Darcy were off in their own little ink-colored world. She had nobody to talk to, so she decided to try to insert herself between D and D again. "Are you really getting a tattoo today, Devon?"

"No," he said. "They're cool, but I'm not into spending all those Benjamins on body art."

"Little tats don't cost so much," Darcy said, and just like that they fell back into an exclusive conversation. Haley realized Darcy was a tougher opponent than she'd thought. Devon had been a little short with Haley, as if he was impatient with her constant interruptions. How dare he? Was he really that into this Darcy chick? And was he done with Haley for good?

With nothing better to do, Haley checked her cell for messages. To her surprise her in-box was flooded with texts, and most of them had the same subject line: "Boob Tubing Babe." Great. The last thing she wanted to think about was the humiliating Hillsdale Hauntings video of her ten-year-old self losing her bathing suit at Lake Tahoe. She skipped all the "Boob Tubing" messages and went straight to the two with nonembarrassing subject lines.

```
Re: Party on
From: Matt Graham
SIGMA @ Eton's pad, just like old
   times. Be there!
```

Huh, Haley thought. Matt Graham? Spencer Eton's friend from boarding school? Haley hadn't heard from him in a while. What made him think of her all of a sudden?

Next she read:

```
Re: Road trip
From: Alex Martin
    Haley, I'm headed up to the
Storm King sculpture gardens this
weekend. It's a beautiful drive.
Want to go?
```

Haley had never been to Storm King, but it was famous for having acres of rolling fields dotted with some of the best examples of modern sculpture in the country. Her father had once mentioned wanting to see it.

With a glance at Devon, who was still deep in some enthralling story with Darcy, Haley announced loudly, "Look at this, Irene. I've got invitations from two different boys for this weekend." If Devon was so intent on flirting with Darcy in front of her, why not go ahead and torture him right back? "Alex Martin wants me to go out of town with him, and Matt Graham is begging me to come to the next SIGMA."

She glanced at Devon to make sure he'd heard. He hadn't. Haley's plan seemed to be backfiring.

"Of course you're popular," Irene said. "They

both probably saw that video of you naked online—like everybody else in school."

Haley's face flushed and she wanted to sink right through the floor. She hadn't thought of that response from Irene. But then, Rini always did like to cut the tall trees down. Of course—all these messages, this sudden burst of attention, was probably just the aftermath of that stupid video.

"Ow!" Shaun cried. Viper was really working the needle on his forearm now. "Ow! Dang it, that hurts! Rini, come back and hold my hand. Viper, dude, why didn't you warn me?"

"Um, I did," Viper said over the whine of the needle.

"You said a *little*," Shaun said. "You said it might hurt a *little*! You didn't say you were going to burn my arm off!"

"Calm down, you'll get through it," Viper said. "Look at me, I've been through this dozens of times and I'm still breathing."

"Hey—remember what I said about the tentacles!" Irene snapped.

Left to herself, Haley glumly watched Irene fuss over Shaun's tattoo while Devon and Darcy talked and laughed. Devon seemed so relaxed with Darcy, and Haley had never seen him so talkative with anyone, certainly not with her. What was it about Darcy that made him so different around her?

"Okay, you're done," Viper finally told Shaun.

Shaun got up groaning from the table. "This better look amazing."

"It will, trust me," Viper said. "Okay, who's next? Irene?"

Irene nodded at Haley. "I'd better nurse Shaun for a few minutes. You want to go?"

Darcy looked over to hear Haley's response. It was almost as if she were saying *I dare you.*

Haley looked at Shaun, overacting a bit but obviously in some pain, and then at her lopsided butterfly drawing. Was she really ready for this?

●　●　●

A tattoo for Haley? That's about as permanent as you can get. Her parents won't be thrilled, but maybe she doesn't care what her parents think anymore. Maybe she's in the mood for a little rebellion, tired of always being the overlooked good girl. Of course, she hasn't been exactly overlooked lately; the "Boob Tubing" video has made her kind of locally famous. Or even infamous. Maybe she should get a tattoo, if only to live up to her new reputation. Then she'd be more like Darcy, and some guys—Devon, for example—seem to find that type very attractive.

Is Haley's newfound reputation as Miss Naked what's really behind the sudden flurry of invitations, or are Alex and Matt seriously interested in her? Alex doesn't seem like the lascivious type, but then, he is a boy, so you never know. Matt Graham is another story, but he doesn't invite just anybody to those SIGMA parties. They're the most exclusive events in town.

If you think Haley is feeling competitive with the tattooed Darcy and is raring to rebel, have her GET THE TAT on page 232. If you think Haley shouldn't even consider getting a tattoo for one second, that she has enough problems to deal with at the moment and is getting plenty of attention already thanks to that video, go to page 238, DON'T DO IT.

Then there are the boys. If you're sure Haley would love to go with Alex to see the sculptures at STORM KING, turn to page 226. If you think Haley would be more interested in seeing the kind of sculptures Spencer and his private-school buddies make with their empty beer cans, turn to OLD HABITS on page 242.

Fate has brought Haley to an impasse: good girl or rebel? Should she go with the flow and give up on her reputation, or should she fight for it tooth and nail?

TEA AND SYMPATHY

Tuxedos do not gentlemen make.

"We're here," Whitney said. "Birthday central."

Sasha pulled up to the De Clerqs' palatial Hillsdale estate, which had been transformed to look like, well, a palatial *English* estate. Haley stepped out of the car and admired the over-the-top decorations. The house was surrounded by gigantic heaters to stave off the new Jersey December chill and create just the right balmy summer atmosphere. *My mom would flip,* Haley thought, glancing at the ginormous kerosene lamps. The house's front columns were draped with garlands of English roses in creamy whites and, in honor of the holidays, a few rich reds. A liveried footman greeted the guests at the door with a tip of his hat, and a maid dressed in nineteenth-century attire led them through the house to the vast formal "gardens," flown in especially for the event. A huge glass conservatory had been erected near the pool, and all the planted paths leading up to it were lined with more gas heaters. Haley knew Coco, of all people, would be able to figure out a way to make it possible for them all to wear sundresses in December.

The double doors of the conservatory opened onto a lavish scene. Skirted tables were laden with platters of tea sandwiches, scones, clotted cream, jams, croissants and a tiered silver tower filled with macaroons, tea cakes and delicate pastries. Earl Grey was served in antique bone china cups with real silver teaspoons and fine linen napkins. Everything was perfect, and gorgeous, including the hostess.

"Hello! Hello! Come in. You brought a gift? You shouldn't have. There's a huge receiving table set up over there for presents." Coco greeted her guests like the princess she was, dressed in an Empire-waist ivory silk Josephine gown. She was in her element, basking in the attention and the glamour, and it suited her.

Haley set her present down next to the towering pile on the gift table. She paused to take in the impressive room. English country flower arrangements bloomed over every table, and braids of blossoms dripped from the chandeliers. The place smelled heavily of cake and perfume. Coco had meticulously attended to every detail, to an almost fanatical degree. If Haley hadn't known it was a mere birthday party, she might have thought this was Coco's wedding/debutante ball.

She was surprised, too, at the number of adults mingling among Coco's school friends. Friends of the Etons, perhaps, Haley thought, or maybe adults invited by Coco to appeal to Mrs. Eton. Eleanor Eton, the future governor herself, was resplendent in an ice blue silk day suit. She was clearly crazy about Coco and led the girl through the room, introducing her to the adults as "the charming birthday girl, my almost daughter and the best thing that's ever happened to Spencer." Coco beamed and practically curtsied at each introduction.

After a few minutes, the string quartet took a break and a dj took over the speakers. A few of the younger guests started dancing, though the music was still pretty staid, much too slow to dance to. They more sort of hugged and slowly rocked back and forth. *Well, here goes,* Haley thought. She couldn't spend the whole party watching from the sidelines. She took a deep breath and plunged into the packed conservatory to mingle.

As she waited for a crystal cup of punch, Haley

heard a girl's voice behind her, whispering her name. Another girl hissed something back and giggled. Haley turned around and caught three well-dressed freshman staring at her and gossiping about the boob tubing fiasco. Her cheeks grew hot. So people were still talking about the video of Haley that was circulating online. She took her punch and looked for someone she knew.

"There you are, Buffy." Spencer Eton, wearing a dove gray suit and holding a glass of "orange juice," slapped Haley rudely on the back so that she almost spilled her drink. "Tally ho."

Haley recoiled from Spencer's eyelash-curling liquor breath. His orange juice was obviously spiked with something a lot stronger than soda water. Spencer confirmed this theory by discreetly pulling a silver flask from his jacket and pouring a little more vodka into his glass. "Seen any good videos lately?" he said, slurring slightly. He wasn't just drinking— he was out and out drunk.

"Not lately," Haley replied. "I'm waiting for your trashy SIGMA videos to end up online." Coco was still busy being squired around by Spencer's mother. Haley felt awkward hanging out with the hostess's drunken boyfriend, but she didn't know who else to talk to. This party was beginning to feel like a field full of land mines—with every step she took, something could blow up in her face.

"Haley, you're looking fine as always." Matt Graham, Spencer's old boarding school friend, kissed Haley on the cheek. "Did somebody say SIGMA? You know we're reviving it this weekend, right? At the Etons' humble abode."

Haley caught Spencer elbowing Matt in the side. He was too drunk to be subtle. "Shut up—I'm not supposed to invite any of Coco's friends," Spencer muttered.

"But dude, it's Haley," Matt said. "We can make an exception."

"No we can't," Spencer said. "No friends of Coco's—not even the boob tuber."

Haley felt like throwing the contents of her crystal glass in his face. The "boob tuber"? How drunk did Spencer have to be to say something that rude to her face?

Horrified, Haley walked away without a word and tried to lose herself in the crowd. She spotted Reese Highland off in a corner near the dessert table. He looked forlorn leaning on his crutches and watching the revelers dance, his left foot still in a cast. *At last,* Haley thought, someone too mannerly to insult her.

"Hide me," she said to Reese. "Everybody in this room has seen me naked—and they won't let me forget it."

Reese grinned. "Poor girl. I'm feeling out of it

myself. But I've got your back. Stay here with me and we'll hide out together."

"Thanks." Haley reached for two chocolate-covered strawberries and gave one to Reese. "At least the food's good."

"Awesome," Reese said. "A whole lot better than the dancing."

Haley laughed. They watched their classmates wriggle on the dance floor in their fancy clothes. Most of them looked like awkward kids at a bad school dance. Then Mia Delgado, dressed in a slinky, low-cut red gown, stepped onto the floor and started swaying by herself.

"That's a different breed, right there," Reese said, and he was right. Tall and sinuous, Mia stood out from everyone else at the party. She moved with sexy confidence. There was nothing awkward or teenagery about her at all.

"Got to give her props, it's a bold move coming in here dressed like that," Haley said.

From a table across the dance floor, Spencer, Matt and their private-school friends sat drinking their spiked juice and laughing loudly. "Mia, Mia," they chanted. Mia ignored them and kept on dancing.

"She's pretty brave," Haley said. She wouldn't have lasted a second on that dance floor by herself, knowing that everyone was talking about her.

"Hook me up, Mia, hook me up, Mia, hook me up . . ." Now Spencer and his friends were yelling louder. Haley thought she saw Mia flinch. She grabbed the hands of a nearby boy and let him twirl her around.

"Hook me up, Mia, hook me up. . . ." The chanting got louder. Finally Mia couldn't take it anymore. She ran out of the ballroom toward the bathroom.

"Rotten stuff," Reese said. "She may never live that video down."

Haley felt nervous. "I probably shouldn't have ever left the house today. Spencer and those guys could do the same thing to me."

"They're thugs," Reese said. "Don't mind them."

"I think I'll get out of here before they get a chance to ruin my night too." Haley said.

"I'll go with you," Reese said. "I'm bored out of my mind." Then, as if realizing he'd said something rude, he added, "Not with you. With the party, I mean."

Haley smiled, for the first time all night. "Let me just make sure my mom knows she doesn't need to pick me up." She opened her clutch purse and peeked at her cell phone. She had twelve new messages. What could that be about?

Scanning through them, she saw that they mostly seemed to be from random boys, some of whose names she didn't even recognize. *The video,* she thought grimly. *This is all because of that stupid video.*

Then she noticed a message from Matt Graham. She glanced across the room and saw him sitting at Spencer's table. Why didn't he just come over and talk to her in person if he had something to say? She opened the message just out of curiosity. It said, "H, Come to SIGMA. XO Matt."

She looked at him again, and this time he caught her eye. He flashed her a sly smile, then winked.

● ● ●

Some party, huh? Coco's ginormous birthday extravaganza was extravagant, all right, but that doesn't always guarantee a good time. Some people seem to be having fun—Coco first and foremost—but Haley isn't sharing the spirit of the occasion. And watching Mia flame out didn't exactly help. Hate to break it to you, Mia, but if you're looking for a blasé Continental attitude, you're going to have to look a lot farther than New Jersey.

At least Reese is behaving himself. That's nice, but not always thrilling. If you think Haley should play it safe and hang with Reese, taking refuge amid all this torturous embarrassment and negative attention, stick with the good guy on page 256, GOING PUBLIC.

Don't forget Matt Graham's persistent invitation to party at SIGMA. Who knows—maybe if Haley parties with the thugs in suits, she'll get them on her good side and they won't tease her about the embarrassing video.

If you think Haley is feeling wild and curious, show up at Spencer's house on page 242, OLD HABITS.

Old habits die hard, they say, but playing it safe has its own risks—namely restlessness and boredom. Which route should Haley take? The first step is up to you.

INVESTIGATE MIA

Even the most explicit video doesn't reveal everything.

Haley couldn't concentrate on her homework. She kept thinking about Whitney Klein's father and Mia Delgado. Was there really something going on between them? Haley couldn't rest until she found the answer. She knew how she'd feel if her own father were involved with someone her age: disgusted. Luckily, Haley's father wasn't that type. At least, as far as she knew. He was surrounded by college girls for half the week. Did Whitney realize her father was a perv? She'd have to be pretty blind not to. But people could be blind when confronted with something they didn't want to see.

Haley logged on to the Internet and went to the Web site for Jerry Klein's company, New Jersey Breath Spray. She knew that Mia had been on Jerry's guest list for a campaign fund-raiser for Governor Eton, so she had a sneaking suspicion that she'd find clues about the nature of their relationship in his e-mail correspondence. Somewhere, Jerry Klein probably had e-mails from Mia. All Haley had to do was find them.

To her surprise, breaking into Mr. Klein's e-mail account was far easier than she'd expected. She was no hacker, but once she'd found his e-mail address through the company Web site and the remote access site, all she had to do was crack his password. She sat back and thought, *What would an obvious password be?* He couldn't be so stupid as to use his name or birthdate. Who else's name would he use? How about his daughter's? Haley typed WHITNEY in the password box but it didn't work. Too easy. Next she tried his new wife's name, Trisha. Access denied. Aha—what if he combined the two names somehow? That would make sense—the names of the two most important females in his life—not counting, possibly, Mia. TrishWhit? No. Whitrish? Haley chuckled as she typed in WHITRISH.

Voila! WHITRISH worked. She was in.

Excited and nervous, Haley got up and double-checked that her bedroom door was locked. She didn't want anyone catching her when she was up to no good. But it was all for a worthy cause, she told herself.

She searched through Mr. Klein's e-mails. He had several private folders, one marked "Trisha," another from his ex-wife, Linda, and several others filled with nothing but boring business exchanges. Then she hit the jackpot: a folder marked with a simple "M." Haley opened it, and sure enough, M stood for Mia Delgado.

Mr. Klein had saved dozens of e-mails from her. Haley shook her head. There had to be something going on between them, or why so much correspondence? She opened the most recent message and read it.

Jerry,
    I'm so sorry to do this, but I must ask for your help. You've done so much for me already, getting me into that fund-raiser the girls at school were excluding me from, I hate to ask, but I'm desperate! I'm being blackmailed by a fashion photographer named Philip Fogelman. We used to date, for a little while, when I was living

in New York, and now I find out
he videotaped some of our, how
you say, encounters? He put a
video of us in bed on the
Internet already! And now he says
he will release more "romantic
footage," even more explicit!
Unless I move back to New York
and start modeling for him again.
I never want to pose for or see
him again! But the only
alternative is to pay him off, and
it requires a lot of money. . . .

Haley couldn't believe her eyes. Mia was asking
Mr. Klein for money to pay off this Philip Fogelman
character and save what was left of her reputation—
Poor Mia, being blackmailed by that icky man—and
having no one else to turn to for help but Jerry Klein.
Haley began to see the glamorous Spanish girl in a
new light. She noticed an attachment at the bottom
of the e-mail. She didn't dare open it—she assumed it
was probably the "romantic footage" Mia was worried about, and that was the last thing Haley wanted
to see.

Her phone beeped and she noticed she had a load
of text messages coming in all at once. Most of them
were from boys she barely knew and carried the annoying subject line "Boob Tubing Babe." She didn't

bother with them and opened the one normal-looking message instead. It was from Matt Graham, a boarding-school buddy of Spencer Eton's. Haley hadn't heard from him in a while and wondered what he could want.

> Come to SIGMA this weekend, at Eton's house. Can't wait to see you again. XO, Matt.

XO? From Matt Graham? That was a surprise.

● ● ●

So, there's more to Mia than meets the eye. But is she telling the truth? Or is she up to something sneaky? If you think finding out the truth about Mia's complicated life has made Haley want to RESCUE MIA, turn to page 248. If you think Haley doesn't need to help this girl gone wild—after all, Mia's made so many foolish decisions on her own, she may be beyond help—LET HER ROT on page 253.

Is Haley less concerned with Mia's problems and more embarrassed about her own online scandal at the moment? Have her try to get over her fear of GOING PUBLIC on page 256. If you think that Haley should forget her troubles and take Matt up on his invite to SIGMA at Spencer's, go party hearty at the boys' hangout on page 242 (OLD HABITS).

GETTING FRESH

Sometimes the truth can be very refreshing.

"Hi, Marta," Whitney Klein said to the secretary at the desk outside her father's office. "Is Dad in?"

"He is, but he's on the phone," Marta said.

"I don't care," Whitney said, marching past the secretary's desk. "We're going in."

"Whitney, wait!" Marta cried, but Whitney ignored her.

"Come on, girls." She waved at Haley and Sasha to follow her.

Haley and Sasha had agreed to go with Whitney

to the corporate headquarters of her father's breath spray company. She needed moral support because her mission was painful: to confront him about the video of Mia Delgado he had stashed on his home computer. Whitney had been shocked to think that her father was obsessed with a girl in her own grade at school, and was determined to confront him about this once and for all.

Whitney barged into her dad's corner office and sure enough, he was on the phone, a conference call. "Whittles, what a pleasant surprise! What's the occasion?"

"I'll tell you what the occasion is," Whitney said, her voice already rising to a shrill pitch. Haley moved quickly to close the door to the office. No need to scandalize everybody in the company.

"You're a pervert!" Whitney shouted.

"Um, gentlemen, I'm going to have to call you back," Jerry said nervously, disconnecting the call.

"You're involved with Mia Delgado! How could you, Dad? First you dump Mom for that bimbo Trisha, and then you start slobbering over a girl in my class?"

Mr. Klein looked stunned for a moment but quickly recovered. "Whittles, honey, what makes you say this? You've got it all wrong—"

"What makes me say it? How about I found that raunchy video of Mia on your computer?" Whitney said. "What are you doing watching filth like that, of a teenaged girl?"

"I'll tell you what I was doing with it," Mr. Klein said. "If you'll all just take a seat and calm down."

"I won't calm down! I won't!" Whitney shouted.

Haley gently led her to a chair and made her sit. "Listen to your dad, Whitney. He might have an explanation."

"I already know the explanation," Whitney said. "My father's a perv! Ew!"

"Whitney, stop," Jerry said firmly. "Now listen. The reason I bookmarked that video is that Mia asked me to help her. The man who posted that footage is a New York fashion photographer she used to work for named Philip Fogelman."

Whitney sat up. "I've heard of him," she said. "We saw him at Bubbies the other day. Love his work."

"Well, I don't," Jerry Klein said. "He and Mia used to be . . . involved, I guess you'd say. And he has a lot of video footage of their . . . involvement. And now he's blackmailing her, saying that he'll post even more explicit pictures and films of her on the Internet if she doesn't do what he wants."

"She's lying," Whitney said matter-of-factly. "Philip Fogelman wouldn't do something so terrible."

"How do you know?" Sasha said. "Do you know him personally?"

"No, I just think, Why would a known photographer have to stoop so low?" Whitney said.

"To get what he wants," Jerry said. "Either Mia goes back to New York to work with him again, or he'll post those videos. And the only other way to stop him is to pay him off. That's why Mia came to me—to borrow the money she needs to make him go away."

"Oh." Whitney looked chastened now and kind of annoyed that she'd have to rethink her opinion of Mia.

"It goes without saying that what I'm telling you girls is confidential, okay?" Mr. Klein said. "Okay, Whitney?"

"Okay," Whitney said.

"Of course," Haley said.

"So, you're not dating Mia?" Whitney said. "Not at all?"

"Not at all, pumpkin," Mr. Klein said. "I've got my beautiful, if demanding, Trisha at home."

Whitney looked relieved, but at the sound of her stepmother's name she couldn't help making a sour face.

"Good," she said to her father. "Keep it that way."

● ● ●

So that explains that. Jerry Klein is not—in this case, anyway—a pervert. And Mia Delgado is not as skanky as she appeared to be, either. In fact, she seems to truly be the victim here.

But has this changed Haley's opinion of her? If you think Haley feels sorry for Mia and wants to help her, go to RESCUE MIA on page 248. If you think Haley still doesn't like her or trust her, no matter what Philip Fogelman is doing to her reputation, LET HER ROT on page 253.

If you think Haley would rather forget all about this online scandal and do a little much-needed partying instead, send her to SIGMA with Matt Graham on page 242 (OLD HABITS).

TOTAL MORTIFICATION

It's not easy to be a hermit
in the burbs.

Haley logged on to her computer for the fifth time in an hour. She went to the Hillsdale Hauntings site and clicked on "Boob Tubing." Yes, it was still there: that horrible vision of her at age ten at Lake Tahoe, riding on an inner tube being pulled by a motorboat. She cringed as the tube crashed through a heavy wake and she lost her bathing suit. There she was again, washing ashore naked. No, it wasn't all just a bad dream.

Why did she keep doing this to herself? She knew the nightmare was real; she just couldn't get her mind around it. It was too horrible to contemplate, yet there it was in living color for the whole school to see.

Ding—another text message came in. She didn't have the heart to even see who it was from. She'd been bombarded for hours with e-mails and texts about the humiliating footage; then she'd locked herself in her bedroom and vowed never to leave. She couldn't take it anymore. How had this happened to her? Well, she knew how. Garrett "the Troll" Knoll had began working at the post house where her father had been transferring all their old home movies to digital. But it didn't make the fact that the most humiliating home video ever shot was now leaked onto the Internet any easier to take. Her life was ruined. All she could do was hide in her room until the scandal died down—if it ever did.

In a way, it was all her dad's fault for taking the videos to an amateur in the first place. If only he were home, she'd go downstairs and yell at him once again for letting their personal footage fall into the wrong hands . . . even though she knew in her heart her dad didn't really deserve to be yelled at. It might help her feel better, that was all.

Her phone beeped again. Five more text messages from random guys with the same subject line: "Boob Tubing Babe." There was one from Matt Graham labeled "Hi Haley," but who knew what he had to say. Matt was a friend of Spencer Eton's and a well-known party guy. She shut her phone off in disgust and threw it onto the desk. She couldn't take it anymore—negative attention overload. She started to tear up and fell onto her bed to settle in for a good cry. Why did this have to happen to her? Just when things were starting to go so well . . .

The doorbell rang. Haley stopped crying and listened. There was no one else home to answer it. She lay still, waiting for whoever it was to go away.

It rang again. And a third time. Who was this annoying, persistent person? Haley got up and went into the hall. She peered through the window and saw Reese Highland standing on the front porch, leaning on his crutches.

Reese. What did he want? Haley wasn't sure she had it in her to hear what Reese had to say on the subject of her public humiliation, but he certainly seemed determined to say something. He rang the bell again, and Haley gave up and decided to let him in.

"Hi," she said when she opened the front door.

"Hi," he said."

"I'm hiding," Haley confessed. "I'm thinking of becoming a hermit when I grow up, so I thought I'd get a head start and practice now."

"Can I come in and be a hermit with you?" Reese asked.

"Sure." Haley let him in. How could she resist an invitation to co-hermit with Reese? "Come on up to the hermit cave."

She got them some tea and they settled down on the rug in her room. "I understand how you feel, but you can't take this so hard," Reese told her. "Have a sense of humor about it. Really, it's not so bad. You got off a lot easier than Mia did."

Haley shuddered. Mia's video showed her making out in bed with an older guy, in her bra. "But that's different. Mia's video is more . . . sexy. At least she doesn't come off like a complete idiot. And she's not totally naked."

"But her video is . . . pretty hard-core," Reese said. "From what I've heard. While yours is innocent and kind of cute."

"Cute?" Haley softened up a little. Reese thought she looked cute?

"Sure," Reese said. "You're just a kid. It's funny. We've all been there."

"Not all over the Internet," Haley said.

"Come on, these things happen all the time in high school."

"What things?"

"Embarrassing things," Reese said. "Haven't you ever heard your parents talk about all the humiliations they suffered when they were younger?"

"Yes, and it gives me nightmares," Haley said. "I don't like to think about it."

"I'm just saying, it happens to everyone sooner or later."

"Not to me," Haley said. "I'm not the naked video type. Except now everyone in school thinks I am. You should see all the texts I've gotten, just in the last few hours! Every boy in Hillsdale wants to see how my body has changed. Up close and personal." She sighed. "I swear, I'm never going out in public again. People are going to give me weird looks and whisper behind my back—"

"So they whisper for a few days—so what?" Reese said. "Lap it up. It's your moment in the sun. Scandal's not what it used to be, you know. Now it's chic. All the celebrities are doing it."

Haley laughed. "That's the spirit," Reese said. "Laugh it off." He was surprisingly good at cheering her up when he put his mind to it.

"Aren't you starting to feel a little claustrophobic in your hermit cave?" Reese said. "I think we need a field trip."

"No way," Haley said. "I'm not going out there."

"Yes you will. Come on, you know you can't stay hidden forever. Will your parents let you skip school for the rest of your life? Didn't think so."

"There's no place to go anyway," Haley said. "No place safe, that is."

"I know a place we can go," Reese said. "And I can almost guarantee nobody we know will be there."

"Where?"

"The public library." Reese grinned. "Let's go right now. You seriously need to get out of here."

Haley had to hand it to him—nobody they knew hung out at the library. It was about as safe a haven as she was going to find in this town.

● ● ●

Good old Reese—it's about time he came through for Haley. He hasn't exactly been there for her lately, but times like these make up for any neglect. Or do they? Is it enough to keep Haley's spirits afloat, or is it just a temporary salve, a slight bandage over a bullet wound? All those text messages crowding Haley's in-box suggest that the problem may be bigger than Reese thinks.

If you believe Reese is right that Haley needs to get out of her house, turn to page 256, GOING PUBLIC. Or maybe Haley should read through the text messages she's received while her phone was shut off. If she does, she'll find a message from Matt Graham inviting her to the next SIGMA bash at Spencer Eton's house. If you think she should forget her troubles by going to a wild party, turn to page 242, OLD HABITS. Finally, if you think suffering through this scandal has given Haley sympathy for Mia Delgado's plight, turn to page 248, RESCUE MIA.

It's usually calm before
a storm, but not when
Dave Metzger is around.

"The house should be on the next block," Dave said from the backseat. "Oh God, I'm so nervous. Look, my underarms are dripping."

Haley glanced back at him from the front seat, then turned away. Why did she want to see Dave Metzger's sweaty underarms? She didn't.

"At least you haven't broken out, sweetie," Annie said, patting Dave. "Not in the last hour, anyway."

Alex, in the driver's seat, gritted his teeth. After hearing that Alex Martin had asked Haley to go to upstate New York to the Storm King Art Center with him, Dave invited himself to come along for the ride. He'd just found out that his estranged father lived in nearby Newburgh. And of course, where Dave went, Annie went too. So it was a road trip, the four of them.

Also against Alex's wishes, Dave had convinced him to stop at his father's house first, before going on to Storm King. Now they were driving through a modest neighborhood in Newburgh, looking for the address Dave had found on the Internet.

"There it is!" Dave shouted. "That's it—1149. Pull over! But not right in front. I don't want him to see me yet."

Alex stopped the car across the street from a modest split-level house painted a rather ugly shade of pale pea green. They sat in the car for a few minutes, just staring at the house. Then the front door opened and a man came out with three young children, elementary school–age, and a woman who appeared to be his wife. The man was dumpy, with a large bald spot at the back of his head, and the woman had teased her blond hair until it looked like a cloud of cotton candy.

"That's him," Dave said. "That's my father."

The family walked to the driveway, where a minivan was parked, and started piling in. Annie nudged Dave. "Go! Get out there and introduce yourself to him!"

Dave sat frozen in his seat, staring at the family he'd never had.

"Come on, Dave," Haley said. "Aren't you going to go say hello?"

"Yeah," Alex said. "Isn't this what we drove all this way for?"

"I can't," Dave said. His father shut the children inside the minivan and got into the driver's seat.

"Hurry up, Dave!" Annie said. "They're about to drive away."

"No," Dave said. His hands were shaking in his lap. "Let's get out of here. Drive away, Alex. Now."

"Whatever you say." Alex pulled away down the street before the minivan left the driveway.

"Why did you do that, Dave?" Annie asked. "Didn't you want to talk to him? Isn't that what we came here for?"

"I don't want to talk about it." Dave moped.

There was an awkward silence in the car as they drove out to Storm King. Haley was relieved when they finally got there. She sprang out of the car. Dave stumbled out like a zombie and wandered blankly into the frozen sculpture garden.

Annie hurried after him. "Dave, wait!"

"It's so good to get out of the car," Haley said to Alex.

"Tell me about it," Alex said. "I'm glad to get a break from Dave's family drama for a while. Come on, I'll show you the grounds."

228

Haley pulled her knit cap over her ears against the frosty air. Dave and Annie had shambled off to the left, so Haley and Alex went right. The frozen ground crunched under her boots as she tramped through the fields. The day was cloudy; in the distance, mountains loomed in a shroud of mist. They walked together in a companionable silence, a kind of intimate not-talking.

Alex stopped in front of a large iron abstract sculpture by Henry Moore. They stared at the rusty metal spheres for a while in silence. Then Alex said, "This sculpture always reminds me of my youngest brother for some reason."

Haley studied it more closely. In what way did this collection of shapes remind Alex of a person? She grinned; this was the most personal thing she'd ever heard Alex say. It was odd, but it humanized him somehow.

"I didn't know you had brothers," Haley said.

"Two, actually," Alex said. "I'm the oldest of three boys. You should come over to the house sometime and meet everybody."

"I'd like that." Haley rubbed her nose, which was starting to go numb. Alex looked at her face just then, and she wondered if he wanted to kiss her. Maybe he'd kiss her right on her cold nose.

But nothing happened, so to fill the silence Haley said, "Feels like snow."

Alex looked up at the sky. "Yeah, it does, doesn't it."

Just kiss him! Haley thought. *Make the first move yourself. Why not?*

Alex looked into her eyes, and Haley decided to go for it. Just as she leaned forward, Annie shouted, "Hey!" and ran over to them.

Too late. Haley would have to try again later.

"Can we leave now?" Annie asked.

"Why?" Alex said. "We just got here."

"I know, but Dave's back in the car and he's really freaking out," Annie said. "Besides, it's freezing and there's a storm headed to Storm King."

Haley felt a cold prickle on her face, and then another. It was starting to snow. Snow! At last! The sky was filling up with dancing white flakes. Haley opened up her mouth and caught the first few of the season on her tongue.

"Well, maybe we should go," Alex said. "I don't have snow tires, so the drive back could be rough if we wait."

"I heard on the radio they're predicting we'll get over a foot tonight," Annie said.

"A foot!" Haley said happily. "That's great!" This was her second winter on the East Coast; her first had been a bust, with not much white stuff on the ground. "I hope I'll get to experience my first real East Coast snow day."

"Me too," Alex said as they walked back to the car. "If we do have off from school, you should come over to my house to go ice-skating. We have a small pond in our backyard and it's already frozen solid."

· · ·

Well, the search for Dave's father was a bust, and Dave didn't handle it very well. He and Annie tagged along on Alex and Haley's date for nothing. What would have happened between Alex and Haley if the other two hadn't been there? Would they have been trapped for the night in Mountainville? We'll never know. But Haley certainly seems to be turned on by sculpture.

To have Haley take Alex up on his invitation to go to his house, go to page 260, HEARTH AND HOME. If you think seeing all the sculptures only made Haley miss hanging out with her favorite artists, Irene, Shaun and Devon, go have a MOVIE MARATHON on page 266. If you are really hoping this snow hits hard, plan to spend this hypothetical snow day with Reese on page 283, LET IT SNOW.

GET THE TAT

Tattoos aren't always
as permanent
as people think.

"**O**kay, guys, who's next?" Viper the tattoo artist asked.

Haley looked from Irene to Devon to Darcy to Shaun, who'd just gotten his tattoo and gave her a thumbs-up. Haley raised her hand and said, "I'll go."

Devon arched an eyebrow and Irene said, "Haley, are you sure?"

"It doesn't wash off, you know," Shaun said. "Even if you scrub."

"I'm positive," Haley said. All afternoon she'd

watched while Darcy bragged about how much she loved the star tattoo on her wrist and Devon listen as if it were the most fascinating conversation on earth. Devon clearly had a thing for girls with tattoos. And if that was the case, Haley was going to become one.

"Will you help me pick out a design, Irene?" Haley asked. "My drawing isn't really good enough. I think I want the Chinese symbol for harmony—on my ankle." She didn't want to have to look at the lame butterfly she'd drawn in Mr. Von's art class for the rest of her life.

"No problem." Irene and Haley flipped through the book of designs until they found the Chinese character for harmony. "It's beautiful," Haley said.

She sat down in Viper's chair and held out her foot. "Show me exactly where you want it," he said. Haley pointed to her ankle bone.

"Nice," Devon said. "That's going to look fierce."

As Viper prepped her ankle, the others gathered around to watch. Devon was impressed with her boldness, she could tell by the look on his face. And how did Darcy feel? Haley wasn't sure, but she had the feeling Darcy was annoyed to lose the spotlight.

"This might hurt a little," Viper said as the needle whined. He applied it to her ankle bone and Haley winced in pain. It really stung. She tried to hide her discomfort.

"Talk to her," Shaun said to the others. "It'll help take her mind off the pain."

So Haley's friends did their best to entertain her while Viper drew the Chinese character on her skin. Haley had to admit she enjoyed the attention. *I should take chances more often,* she thought.

When he was finished, Viper taped a thick layer of gauze over the tattoo and told Haley to leave the bandage on overnight. "Take it off carefully tomorrow, and whatever you do, don't pick at the scab."

Irene went next, and she didn't hide the pain as well as Haley had. "Shaun, why didn't you warn me about this?" she said with a grimace. "It feels like I'm scratching a bad sunburn. A really bad one."

"I did warn you, babe," Shaun said. "But don't worry, it's totally worth it."

Haley sat next to Devon, watching Irene submit to Viper's needle as if she were getting a tooth pulled. Devon nodded at the bandage on Haley's ankle and said, "I bet you can't wait to see how it looks."

"Totally," Haley said. *It will be amazing,* she thought, *and I'll show it to Devon every chance I get. Maybe I'll start wearing more short skirts and ankle bracelets.*

When they were all finished, it was time to pay. Whoops. Haley hadn't thought that far ahead.

"That's two hundred dollars for you," Viper said to Shaun. "And one-fifty for each of you girls," he said to Irene and Haley. "Since your tattoos were smaller."

Shaun got out his parents' credit card and Irene, who'd been saving up her restaurant tips for this, counted out her cash.

Haley swallowed hard. She didn't have a hundred and fifty dollars to spend on a tattoo—and she had only forty dollars on her. But she did have the "emergencies only" credit card her dad had given her.

This is an emergency, she reasoned. *I've already gotten a tattoo and I don't have the money to pay for it. Who knows what this guy Viper will do to me if I don't pay?*

So she got out the card, handed it over to Viper and watched with a knot in her stomach as he ran it through his machine.

It'll be okay, she told herself. *I'll think of something to tell Mom and Dad before the bill arrives.*

When she walked through the door an hour later, her parents were waiting for her, and they looked angry. Her mother immediately spotted the bandage on Haley's ankle and cried, "That's it, isn't it? That's a tattoo!"

"A tattoo?" Perry said. "Haley, how could you do that without asking our permission?"

"And then make us pay for it," Joan said. "It's outrageous! I can't believe you'd do such a thing. What's the matter with you?"

Haley was stunned. "How did you find out?"

"The credit card company called," Joan said. "They said someone had used our card to charge something at 'Tommy's Tattoos' and they wanted to double-check with us."

"We told them we had no idea who could have done that," Perry said. "We thought maybe someone had stolen your card. We were afraid you'd been robbed."

"I wasn't robbed," Haley said. "I just went with my friends to the tattoo place and it looked cool so I decided to get one. I had no idea it would be so expensive."

Joan and Perry stared at her in shock. "Where's my sensible, levelheaded daughter?" Joan said. "Do you know what could have happened to you? If this Tommy's place isn't clean you could have picked up hepatitis or any number of diseases. Not to mention you didn't think clearly enough to even inquire about the cost before letting a complete stranger draw on you with a needle!"

"This really shows poor thinking, Haley," Perry said. "I'm sorry, but you're going to have to be punished for this."

"What? I didn't do anything wrong," Haley said. "I'll pay you back for the tattoo."

"Yes, you will," Joan said. "You will also be grounded for your entire holiday vacation. And your only Christmas present this year will be the immediate removal of that tattoo."

・ ・ ・

Haley's parents kept their word. She had to spend the entire Christmas break trapped in the house with her parents and Mitchell, missing all the holiday parties. She received no Christmas presents, not even a pair of socks. And as soon as possible her parents took her to a dermatologist to get her tattoo removed. Little did Haley know that having a tattoo removed hurts even more than getting one—but then she sure found out the hard way.

Hang your head and go back to page 1.

DON'T DO IT

When all the rebels have tattoos, the nonconformist thing to do is to *not* get inked.

"**W**ho's next?" Viper the tattoo guy asked, revving up his electric needle. Haley looked from Irene to Devon to Darcy to Shaun, who had just gotten an octopus etched onto his forearm. Viper pointed the needle at Haley. "How about you, Red?"

Haley shook her head. She had no interest in getting a tattoo. It wasn't her style, and besides, she didn't have the money. "You can go next, Irene," she said. "I think I'll pass on the whole tattoo thing."

"Okay," Irene said. "I'm ready to be marked for life." She handed Viper her ribbon-and-barbed-wire design and settled into his chair.

"This might hurt a little," Viper said.

"Shaun!" Irene cried before Viper even had a chance to touch her.

Shaun held her hand. "Don't worry, Rini, I'm here. Just think happy thoughts. Think about big, beautiful tattoos!"

"You're not helping, Shaun."

Viper went to work, and Irene grimaced in pain. *That looks like it really hurts,* Haley thought, feeling sure she'd made the right decision. To help distract Irene, Haley said, "Did you hear we're supposed to get a big snowstorm tonight? The weather guy predicted we'll get a foot of snow." This would be Haley's first big snowstorm since moving east from California last year, so she was pretty excited about it.

"Snow day tomorrow," Irene said. "I've got a math quiz I haven't studied for, and now I won't have to. Awesome."

"If we get off from school tomorrow, I'll host a movie marathon at my house," Shaun promised, squeezing Irene's hand. "Would you like that, Rini?"

Irene nodded, the pain having rendered her temporarily unable to speak.

"Only three days until winter break," Devon said. "Wouldn't it be awesome if we got the next three days off because of snow? That would mean winter break starts right now."

"Wicked," Darcy said, high-fiving Devon. "Then, if it would just snow at the end of winter break and cancel the first week of school in January . . ."

Haley's cell phone had been buzzing all afternoon, so she finally pulled it out of her pocket to check her messages. She had a bunch of new voice mails and texts about the possibility of a snow day and how to spend the time off. Alex Martin invited her to come to his house and go ice-skating on the pond in his backyard, and Cecily Watson told Haley a bunch of people were getting together at Matt Graham's house for some touch football on the slippery lawn.

● ● ●

So Haley has opted out of the tattoo game, and she's glad to miss the pain, the scabbing and the screaming from her parents if they knew how much it cost. Good move. Now the question is, how to spend a snow day?

If you want to go have a MOVIE MARATHON with this tattooed crowd, go to page 266. If you think Haley has had enough rebellion for a while and would rather go ice-skating on Alex's pond—something she never got to do in California—turn to page 260, HEARTH AND HOME. If you think Haley loves the idea of a snowy day outside playing TOUCH FOOTBALL with Cecily and a pack of cute boys, go to page 271.

Never trust a fox in a henhouse, and never trust a Spencer in a room full of liquor, gambling and girls.

Haley hesitated before knocking on the door of Spencer Eton's house in Hillsdale. The SIGMA party was being held there while Spencer's mother, the governor, was busy with business in Newark and Princeton. It was the perfect setup for Spencer: a luxurious house all to himself where he could get up to all kinds of mischief. And he'd even sent the security detail away, claiming he was just enjoying a quite night at home.

Still, Haley felt funny about being there. She'd

been invited—Spencer's friend Matthew Graham had sent her a text message—but she couldn't help but wonder if the invitation had just been a mass forwarded message sent to every girl in Matt's phone book. In which case, Spencer might not be so happy to see her.

She took a deep breath and knocked. She'd gotten this far; might as well go all the way. Spencer opened the door stinking of vodka, his eyes bloodshot, and swaying in the doorway.

"Haley," he said without enthusiasm. "Great. Who invited you?"

He was about to slam the door in her face without even waiting for her answer, but Matt stepped in at the last minute.

"I invited her, dude," Matt said. "Let her in."

Spencer shrugged and said, "You're an idiot." Then he stabbed a finger in Haley's face. "Before you come in you have to swear not to say one word to Coco about this. Swear?"

"I swear," Haley said.

"Okay." Spencer stepped aside. "You may enter the sanctuary." He turned to Matt and added, "You owe me one."

Haley followed the boys into the dimly lit basement. Spencer's old private school buddies, Max, Jake and Todd, were smoking and drinking around a giant flat-screen TV that had a football game on the main screen and basketball in the pop-up window.

They were glued to the games because they'd all placed hefty bets on the outcomes. A gaggle of giggling girls from St. Agnes, the local Catholic girls' school, surrounded the boys and flirted the way only boy-starved, girls'-school girls can.

Haley couldn't believe her eyes, though she knew she should have expected this. No wonder Spencer had sworn her to secrecy. What would Coco think if she knew her boyfriend was gambling on sports games behind her back, and surrounding himself with a harem of St. Agnes chicks?

"You like vodka and cranberry, right?" Matt put a tall glass of pink alcohol in her hand. "Sure you do. All girls like that."

"Thanks," Haley said. She actually didn't like vodka and cranberry, but she figured there was no harm in just holding the drink. At least that would keep Matt from giving her another one.

She was still wondering exactly why Matt had invited her, since she didn't see any other girls from Hillsdale around. Could it be that he had a crush on her? What other explanation was there? She looked at his profile while he watched the Dallas Cowboys fumble the ball. She didn't know him well, but he was very good-looking, with an air of money and taste about him. When the play was over he smacked his fist into his hand, then turned to Haley and smiled. Wow. What a very melty smile that boy had.

"I've got fifty on the Cowboys, so I don't like to see those fumbles," he said.

"They're still up by ten," Haley said.

"Yeah, there's that." He touched her drink hand lightly. "How's that drink?"

"Good," Haley said, though she hadn't tasted it.

"Good," Matt said. "Just let me know if I can get you anything else."

"Thanks."

Haley was relieved to see Cecily Watson and her boyfriend, Drew Napolitano, come downstairs a few minutes later. At last, someone to talk to. She ran over to say hello.

"What's up?" Cecily said. "I'm glad to see someone here besides those kilt-wearing floozies." She nodded toward a clutch of St. Agnes girls draping themselves over the boys' laps. "I really needed a night out. I've been working long weekends because it's been so busy at the nursery." Cecily's parents owned a green lot that sold Christmas trees and wreaths during the holidays.

"You might be getting a day off tomorrow," Drew said. "I heard it's supposed to snow a foot tonight."

"I hope they cancel school," Haley said.

"Me too," Cecily said.

"If we have a snow day, we're playing touch football at Matt's tomorrow afternoon," Drew said. "Right, Matt?"

"Fine by me," Matt called back from his spot on the leather couch.

"You should come too," Cecily said to Haley. "It'll be fun."

"What about Sasha and Whitney?" Haley asked.

"Oh, those two homebodies," Cecily said. "Sasha told me if we have a snow day they're going to lounge around watching movies. Come play football. It'll be fun."

"If we get the day off," Haley said.

"We will," Drew said. "I can feel it in the air."

Haley was distracted by the sight of a brunette St. Agnes girl flirting shamelessly with Spencer. "Nice house," the brunette said to him. "At least, the basement is nice. I bet the rest of the house is even nicer."

"It is," Spencer said. "Want a tour?"

"More than I've ever wanted anything," the brunette said flirtatiously.

Haley rolled her eyes. What a line.

"Come on." Spencer took the girl's hand and led her upstairs.

"I can't believe he's doing that," Haley said to Cecily.

"You're surprised?" Cecily said. "You know what a jerk he can be. And so does Coco. But she loves him anyway. Drew on the other hand, I ever catch my boy doing that, he's toast."

"It's just that I thought Spencer had reformed. For Coco. And his mom."

"Please," Cecily said. "Spencer is incapable of reform. He's bad to the bone."

● ● ●

Spencer is up to his old tricks again. If Coco knew, she'd be horrified. But there's no way she can find out—or is there? The only person who might tell her is Haley, and she swore to Spencer she wouldn't. But does a promise count when you're dealing with a lowlife Eton? That is the question.

Maybe Haley would rather stay out of Spencer's business and focus on the happy prospect of a snow day instead. If you think Haley should stick with Cecily and keep hanging around Matt Graham to find out exactly why he's interested in her lately, hope for the snow day and a sporty game of TOUCH FOOTBALL on page 271. If you think she'd rather stay toasty warm indoors with Sasha and Whitney, just hanging with the girls, go to page 278, ALL ABOUT AUDREY. If you think Haley owes it to Coco to call her and let her know what her boyfriend is up to behind her back, turn to page 275, SPIES LIKE US. Finally, if this sloppy, sordid scene is making Haley long for wholesome Reese, turn to page 283, LET IT SNOW.

Even supermodels
get the blues.

Haley couldn't stop thinking about Mia's dilemma. No matter what the Spanish model had done in the past, it wasn't right that she was being blackmailed by a photographer, someone who had power over her life and career. And Haley felt terrible for Mia that she had no one to turn to for help besides Whitney's father, Jerry Klein. For all Haley knew Mr. Klein could be a perfectly upstanding citizen, but he clearly enjoyed the company of younger women, and might also be the kind of person to take advantage of a girl in need. *Mia shouldn't have to risk that,* Haley thought.

So Haley called Mia and invited her over to her house. "I heard about the situation you're in, and there's a way out of it that doesn't involve borrowing a dime from Mr. Klein."

"Why should I trust you?" Mia said. "Perhaps you just want me to tell you more personal secrets about my life so you can spread rumors about me all over school like you did last year."

"No, Mia, I swear," Haley said. "I want to help you, and I know I can. Come to my house this afternoon. Whitney and Sasha will be there too."

Mia sounded wary at first, but Haley could hear desperation in her voice too, and at last she gave in. Sasha drove Whitney and Haley to the Millers' house after school. Haley's mother, Joan, had come home from work early and was waiting for them.

"Thanks for helping with this, Mom," Haley said.

"I'm happy to do it," Joan said. "I hate to think of a grown man exploiting an underage girl this way. If any one of you ever got yourself into a situation like this, not that you will, I hope you'd feel free to come to me for help."

"Thanks, Mrs. Miller," Sasha said. "We will."

"Your mom is so cool," Whitney said.

"I just hope Mia will show up," Haley said. She was already fifteen minutes late. She'd refused a ride from Sasha and insisted on coming on her own.

"I hope so too," Joan said.

Haley brewed some tea while they waited. "It's so cold out today. I heard it might snow."

"We're getting a foot!" Whitney said. "Snow day!"

"That would be awesome," Haley said. "I haven't had a real snow day since we moved here."

"Unfortunately, no matter how much we get tonight I still have to go to work tomorrow," Joan said as the doorbell rang and Mia arrived.

"I'm sorry I'm late," she offered.

"It's nice to meet you, Mia," Joan said. "Let's get to work." She led the girls into the kitchen, and over steaming cups of herbal tea they drafted a letter to Philip Fogelman on Joan's law firm's letterhead.

```
Dear Mr. Fogelman:
    I am Mia Delgado's legal
representative. She has told me
of your attempts to blackmail
her. Cease and desist immediately
or we will press charges and file
for a restraining order against
you. We demand that you stop all
communication with my client,
remove all photos of her from the
Internet, and refrain from
posting or publicly displaying
her image in any form without her
```

```
permission. If you do not
comply, in addition to going
to the authorities we will have
no choice but to sue you for
blackmail, defamation, corruption
of a minor, statutory rape, and
child pornography.
    Sincerely,
    Joan Miller, LLD
    Armstrong & White,
Attorneys-at-Law
```

"That ought to scare the scumbag off," Sasha said.

"And if it doesn't, you let me know," Joan said. "And we'll take further action."

"Thank you so much, Mrs. Miller." Mia hugged Joan. "You saved my life."

"Call me Joan," Joan said. "After all, I'm now your attorney."

"Thanks, Mom," Haley said. She felt so proud of her mother.

"Anytime, honey."

● ● ●

Whew. That takes care of that. It was good of Haley to remember that Mia is far from home and on her own. She's sure to earn a lot of good karma from helping Mia this way.

Now, after all that drama, Haley could probably use some downtime—and she deserves some fun. If you think it would be nice of Haley, Sasha and Whitney to include Mia in their snowbound movie marathon, go to page 278, ALL ABOUT AUDREY. If you think Haley would rather make a snow angel or two with Reese once the big storm hits, LET IT SNOW on page 283. If you'd rather see Haley spend her snow day playing TOUCH FOOTBALL with Cecily and the boys, go to page 271.

LET HER ROT

Selfishness has a funny
way of depriving you of
what you want.

"Mia's in big trouble," Sasha said. "Maybe we should think of a way to help her out."

"Yeah," Whitney said. "A way that doesn't involve my dad."

Haley had just found out that Mia Delgado had asked Whitney's father, Jerry Klein, to lend her money to pay off fashion photographer Philip Fogelman. The skanky Mr. Fogelman was threatening to post more humiliating sex videos of Mia on the Internet if she didn't come work for him—or pay up.

"I don't see any easy way to get her out of this," Haley said, without giving the matter much thought. "The thing is, Mia's not worth it. She got herself into this. If she didn't sleep around, she wouldn't have this problem."

"I guess you're right," Whitney said. "I just wish my dad didn't have to use my future inheritance to pay off this jerk."

So the girls said nothing and watched from the sidelines as Mr. Klein withdrew a large sum from his bank account and gave it to Mia. She paid Philip Fogelman and thought the whole scandal was over. No such luck.

When Philip Fogelman saw how quickly Mia had raised the money, he came right back and demanded more.

"That's it," Mr. Klein said. "I'm hiring a lawyer to deal with this guy." But before he had a chance to do that, Philip Fogelman posted a whole new series of provocative photos and videos of Mia on the Internet. Mia was devastated.

Haley saw Mia's close friend Sebastian Bodega at school the next day. The Spanish hottie was a star of the Hillsdale swim team, and Haley had always had a little thing for him. But he looked tired and upset.

"I saw those pictures of Mia and that photographer," he told Haley. "Disgusting! I can't stand to look at my Mia anymore. It's too painful. So I am leaving. I'm leaving Hillsdale forever and going home to Seville. I hope she stays here so I never have to see her again."

Haley felt terrible. She didn't realize Mia's fate in Hillsdale was so closely tied to Sebastian's. Hillsdale's swim team would never recover from the loss of its star. And, Haley was beginning to see, she might not recover from the loss either. She didn't realize until he was gone how much she liked Sebastian, and how much his presence meant to her. She'd hoped that someday they could be closer, but now that he was gone for good, that was impossible.

● ● ●

Hang your head and go back to page 1.

GOING PUBLIC

During times of stress, slow down.

"Come on, Haley," Reese said. He'd been hanging out in her room for hours, trying to coax her to show her face in public again after the release of her humiliating "Boob Tubing" video. "You can't stay in your room forever. That silly video is from the past, and people don't care about it nearly as much as you think."

Haley lifted the pillow off her face. "I just know everybody is laughing about it behind my back—or worse."

"No they're not," Reese said. "Trust me, that video will be forgotten in a flash. Let's get out of here and go study at the library. We won't see anyone we know there."

"That's for sure." When Haley thought about it, maybe the public library wasn't such a bad idea. She was getting a little sick of staring at the walls of her room. And it was nice of Reese to care.

"All right," she said. "Let's go."

On their way out the door, Mitchell stopped them, wearing his winter coat. "Can I come with you?"

Haley looked at Reese. "Do you mind? It's nice to see him showing an interest in books instead of video games for a change."

"No problem," Reese said. "Let's go, buddy."

"Dad, we're taking Mitchell with us!" Haley called.

"Great! Thanks, Haley," her father replied.

They walked to the town library and headed straight for the kids' section—partly for Mitchell's sake, and partly because Haley knew there was even less chance of running into one of her schoolmates among the picture books.

Mitchell scanned the shelves while Reese and Haley settled down at a tiny little table to study. Haley's cell phone rang, and she switched it to Vibrate. She was getting a text every half hour from some random boy about the famous Boob Tubing video. She tried to ignore it, but her phone kept buzzing. Texts were pouring in, all commenting on the footage.

Great, she thought. *I can't escape, even at the library.*

Mitchell reappeared. "Haley, can you help me? I'm looking for a book about spaceships."

"I'll help you, Mitchell," Reese said. He got up and took Mitchell to the stacks.

Haley seized that moment of privacy to scan the incoming messages. One of them was from Alex Martin, and the subject line was "Ice-skating." At least it didn't say "Boob Tubing Babe," so she opened it.

"Major snowstorm coming," Alex wrote. "I predict a snow day. Want to come to my house and ice-skate if we're off tomorrow? Annie and Dave will be there too."

Haley glanced across the room. Reese pulled a book from the shelves and gave it to Mitchell. Very sweet. She smiled. That broken ankle had slowed him down a bit, after all—in the best possible way.

Outside, the first snowflakes were falling. Alex was right—a big storm was on its way.

● ● ●

Just when we think Reese is too self-centered for our Haley, he turns around and does something sweet like this: coaxing Haley out of her room and helping Mitchell

find a book. If you think Haley completely adores Reese, stick close to home on page 283, LET IT SNOW.

Reese can run hot and cold, however, and Haley should know that by now. It's not always smart to put all your eggs in one basket. If you think she's curious about Alex Martin's invitation—maybe she can't resist the romantic idea of ice-skating on his backyard pond—go to page 260, HEARTH AND HOME.

Finally, if you think the best way to spend a snowy day is with girls only, watching movies, turn to page 278, ALL ABOUT AUDREY.

HEARTH AND HOME

Meeting a guy's family for the first time can be as risky as skating on thin ice.

Haley woke up to the sound of a loud siren—the fire whistles were blowing. She jumped out of bed and ran to the window. Her dream had come true: it had snowed overnight. Almost a foot! Surely schools were closed. Trees and houses and cars were all blanketed in white, which brought a hush over the neighborhood. She'd never seen anything so beautiful.

She pulled on thick socks, two pairs of jeans, a turtleneck sweater and her warmest jacket. She ran downstairs, where her father was scrambling eggs.

"Can I get a ride to Alex's house?" she asked. "He invited me over to go ice-skating."

"I'm going into work late today," Joan said. "I'll drop you off on the way."

"Great! I'll be ready in a minute." Haley put on her snow boots and went into the garage to get her old ice skates. She'd skated before, plenty of times, but always on an indoor rink. She'd never been ice-skating on someone's pond before, and the idea of spending a snowy day with Alex instead of at school was just thrilling.

Joan dropped Haley off in front of the Martins' traditional gray shingle colonial house, surrounded by tall pine trees. Haley slung her skates over her shoulder and walked down the long snowy driveway and around the house to the lovely frozen pond in the back. Alex, Annie, Dave and two younger boys were already skittering happily over the ice.

"Haley! You made it!" Alex skated over to her and hugged her hello. "Here, I'll help you put on your skates."

He brushed some snow off a bench and Haley sat down to change her shoes. Then she glided onto the pond. It took a few laps to get her legs to stop wobbling, but soon she was keeping up with Alex, who grabbed her mittened hands and swung her around. Dave wobbled into them and fell on his butt. Annie skated over to help him up.

"That's fall number four," Dave said.

"He's going for a record," Annie joked.

Alex introduced Haley to the two younger boys zipping easily across the ice. "These are my brothers, Christian and Calvin."

"Hello." Christian appeared to be about ten, and Calvin, who looked like a mini-Alex, was about the same size as Haley's brother, Mitchell.

"How old are you, Calvin?" Haley asked.

"Seven," Calvin said.

"My brother's your age. Do you know him? His name is Mitchell Miller."

"Sure, I know him," Calvin said. "He's sort of a freak." Calvin skated away, saying, "My. Name. Is. Mitchell. I. Am. A. Freak."

Haley flinched. She tried to blow it off, but Calvin's insult stung. Until recently Mitchell had a habit of talking like a robot, and Calvin was making fun of him.

Poor Mitchell, Haley thought, imagining how hard it must be for her sensitive little brother to deal with such an obnoxious boy at school. She felt like belting Calvin with a snowball, but realized she couldn't do that to a little kid. He was probably just following the other boys in his grade. He didn't look like a bully.

They skated and threw snowballs for a couple of hours until they were too cold and wanted to go inside. In the Martins' warm kitchen, Alex's mother had steaming mugs of hot cocoa ready and waiting for all the kids.

"Mom, I'd like you to meet my friend Haley," Alex said. "You already know Annie and Dave, of course."

"Of course," Mrs. Martin said. "I know all the good students at your school, Alex. Hello, Haley. Here's some cocoa."

She gave Haley a mug and sent the kids into the den, where a fire crackled in the fireplace. Haley thought Mrs. Martin's greeting could have been warmer. Was she implying that Haley wasn't a good student? How could she possibly know?

Maybe Alex's mother doesn't like the idea of her son spending time with a girl, Haley thought. *That, or she's always uptight.* Either was a bad opinion.

"How's the ice?" Alex's father, Peter, walked into the den wearing a white lab coat and a stethoscope around his neck. He had glasses and a nice head of thick, glossy hair.

"The pond is perfect, Dad," Alex said. "You should come out for a game of ice hockey."

"Wish I could, Alex, but I've got to get to the hospital," Dr. Martin said. "Enjoy your snow day!"

Interesting, Haley thought. *Alex gets his conservative, uptight tendencies from his mom, and his intellectual, good-hearted side from his dad.* His brother Calvin seemed to take after snippy

Mom, while the jury was still out on quiet Christian.

"Now that it's snowed, it finally feels like Christmas is coming," Annie said.

"I can't wait to give you your present, Haley," Alex said.

Haley put down her mug in surprise. Alex had gotten her a Christmas present? It hadn't even occurred to her to get him one. But it would have been rude to let him know that, so she bluffed.

"I haven't gotten your gift yet," she said. "But I know what it is, and I think you'll really like it." *Now if I can just think of something good to get him . . .*

"I can't wait for all the holiday parties," Annie said. "I hear Sasha Lewis is throwing a big bash at her mom's house, with a live jazz band. Doesn't that sound fun? I hope she invites me."

"I'm sure she'll invite all of us," Haley said. "Sasha's not a snob like Coco."

● ● ●

So, Alex has already gotten Haley a Christmas present. He must really like her. Boys don't buy gifts for no reason. Too bad his mother seems like the disapproving type. How much more of her do you think Haley can stand? And what about the bratty little brother?

If you think Haley should get Alex a Christmas gift so that she's not in the awkward position of receiving with nothing to give in return, go to GIFT SWAP on page

264

287. If you think Haley would much rather avoid the Martin clan and buy Devon McKnight a gift instead, turn to page 293, PRESENT TENSE. Finally, if you think Haley definitely should swing by Sasha's holiday fete, go UNDER THE MISTLETOE on page 306.

MOVIE MARATHON

**Two's company,
three's a crowd,
four's a double date,
and five is just awkward.**

"Rini, this octopus is genius." Shaun leaned against the steel counter in his parents' modern kitchen and admired his new tattoo. "I love him! I call him Octopus Prime." He flexed his bicep, then waved his tattooed forearm for all to see. "Octopus Prime! All bow before him!"

"I'm glad I went with the armband style," Irene said. Even though it was snowing outside, she wore a T-shirt with sleeves cut off at the shoulders to show off her tattoo: a satiny red ribbon interlaced with barbed wire. "Tough yet feminine."

Haley put a bowl of popcorn into the microwave and pressed the Start button. She gazed out the large glass windows into the Willkommens' backyard. It had been snowing since the night before, eight inches already, and the snow was coming down harder than before now. Her long-wished-for snow day had come at last.

"If this keeps up they could cancel school for the rest of the week," she said.

"Which would mean no school until after the holiday break!" Irene said. Their holiday vacation was only two days away. If only it would keep snowing, they could have three whole weeks off from school.

"Which would so rock," Shaun said. "Though I have to say I'm looking forward to introducing Octopus Prime to the student body. I could parade him through the courtyard, then cut all my classes."

"Octopus Prime will still be there in January," Irene said. "He's going to be there for the rest of your life. Good thing you like him."

"I love him!" Shaun roared.

Haley stirred water into a powdery brownie mix. "Devon's late. I wonder if he got stuck in the snow."

The doorbell rang. "That's got to be the Dev-ster. I'll get it!" Shaun barreled down the stairs and opened the front door. A few seconds later he ushered Devon into the kitchen—but Devon wasn't alone. Devon's shadow, Darcy Podowski, aka the fifth wheel, was with him once again. Haley couldn't remember the last time she had seen Devon without the blond freshman. It was getting old. Fast.

Everyone else seemed happy to see her, however. "Hey Darce," Irene said, displaying her tattoo for the newcomers to see. "Check it out. All healed."

"Nice," Darcy said. "You're going to be so glad you got it, Irene. It's like this really cool way of telling the world, This is who I am, man. Deal with it."

Haley turned away so that no one could see her roll her eyes. She took the popcorn out of the microwave and put the pan of brownie batter in the oven.

"Time for the movie marathon," Shaun said. "Everybody downstairs. Bring the popcorn. Take the cannoli."

They settled on the orange L-shaped couches in the media room. "Everybody comfy? Okay. The first movie, well three movies, in the Shaun Willkommen Snow Day Movie Marathon is a classic. The Godfather trilogy."

Irene groaned. "Again?"

He started the first film on the large flat-screen TV. Haley would have enjoyed it more if she could have stopped peeking at Devon and Darcy, who sat together. Were their hands touching? Were they playing footsie? It was driving her crazy.

Haley's cell buzzed in the middle of the movie. She pulled it out of her pocket and discreetly checked the message. It was from Coco De Clerq: "Don't go to Sasha's Christmas Eve party. Come to my house instead—amazing double date w/Spencer & Matt."

That's odd, Haley thought. A double date? With Matt Graham? What was Coco up to?

Across the room, Devon and Darcy giggled. Haley sighed. She thought of Darcy as the fifth wheel, but the truth was that Haley was the fifth wheel here.

● ● ●

So are Devon and Darcy a romantic thing or not? Is Devon that annoying type who likes to keep things "loose"—in other words, vague and undefined? Maybe what he needs is a nudge—or a shove—in the right direction. If you think Haley should get Devon something special for Christmas to show she really cares, turn to page 293, PRESENT TENSE.

Maybe you think that ship has sailed and Haley should move on. What about Matt Graham? No question he's cute, but is that enough for Haley? If you think she should find out what Coco's double-date plan is all about, go to page 301, HOME ALONE.

Finally, if you think Haley should forget both boys and spend Christmas Eve at Sasha's festive party, turn to page 306, UNDER THE MISTLETOE.

TOUCH FOOTBALL

If you want to play, you've got to pay.

When Haley woke up, her room seemed strangely quiet. She looked out the window and—miracle of miracles!—she saw a winter wonderland. The snow was more than a foot deep. Even the roads were covered. School was most definitely canceled!

She dressed in thick socks, snow boots, corduroys, a ski jacket and hat—perfect gear for playing touch football. After twenty minutes of convincing arguments, her mother agreed to drop her off in front of Matt's large stone house on a beautiful, rolling slice of the Hillsdale Heights. "I'm so glad I let your father talk me into this hybrid SUV," Joan confided as the car skidded a little but basically kept her in control.

At Matt's, there was a whole crew of workers stringing Christmas lights along the roof and in the maple trees in front of the house. A team of house-keepers was hanging wreaths and holly leaves in the windows inside.

"Beautiful decorations," Joan said. "But what a waste." The Millers usually made do with a single wreath on the front door.

Haley jumped out of the car and headed to the backyard, where the football game was already in progress.

"Haley, you made it!" Cecily waved to her from her side of the scrimmage line. She was teamed up with Drew and Matt and two preppy boys. Spencer was on the other team with a few of his other boarding-school friends, Max, Jake and Todd.

"Haley's on our team," Matt announced.

"No way, you've already got five," Spencer said. "Haley's with us." He turned to Haley and added, "No kidding around now—we play serious touch football. You with me?"

"Got it." Haley joined Spencer's team and jumped right into the game. On the first play she caught a pass for a first down. She ran the ball and missed Cecily's block. Near the end of the game Spencer handed the ball off to Haley, who faked out Cecily and Drew and ran deep. She sprinted full speed, bobbing and weaving between the boys on the other team. Luckily, she had good speed thanks to stints on the track and soccer teams. The end zone was in sight. She was going to make a touchdown! But just before she got there Matt tackled her into a snowbank. They rolled around in the snow together, fighting over the ball until it rolled into a drift.

Haley sat up, laughing, with snow in her face and hair and down the front of her jacket. "I thought this was touch football," she said. "As in no tackling?"

"The rules change when you play with girls," Matt said. "With girls there's always tackling."

The ball was out of bounds, and Haley's team scored on the next play. Twenty minutes later, she was shivering, wet with melted snow. Her fingers were numb.

"You look like you're freezing," Matt said. "Why don't I take you inside to warm up? The others can play without us."

● ● ●

Haley should certainly go inside and get warm; the question is, how does Matt define "warming up"? If you think she should let Matt help her kill that chill, turn to UP FOR GRABS on page 298.

If you think Haley's had enough and is ready to go

home and spend Christmas Eve with her cute neighbor, one Reese Highland, turn to page 311, HIGH HOLIDAY. Finally, if you think Haley is more interested in attending Sasha's holiday bash, where everyone will be all dressed up in festive party clothes, go to page 306, UNDER THE MISTLETOE.

The line between truth-teller and tattletale is as thin as a razor and cuts like one too.

It's my moral duty, Haley decided. *Spencer Eton is up to no good, and as Coco's friend I've got to let her know.*

She sneaked away from the SIGMA party in the basement and slipped into an upstairs bathroom, where she locked the door and dialed Coco on her cell phone.

"What's up?" Coco said.

"I'm at Spencer's house," Haley whispered. "You're not going to believe what's going on here."

"Say no more," Coco said. "I'll be right there."

She hung up, leaving Haley thinking, *Uh-oh. What have I done?*

Haley stayed in the bathroom, afraid to come out. Forty minutes later she heard the front door burst open. She ran to the hall and peered down into the foyer. Coco had arrived, and she wasn't alone. She'd brought Spencer's mother, the governor of New Jersey, with her. And they both looked like they were ready to kill. They marched down to the basement, while Haley crept downstairs and sneaked out the front door. Before she left she heard Spencer's voice drift up the stairs. "Coco . . . Mother . . . What are you doing here?"

"Everybody out—now!" Mrs. Eton said sternly.

Haley watched the aftermath on the Internet the next day. Someone at the party had a digital camera and posted pictures on the Hillsdale Hauntings Web site for all to see. There were shots of kids smoking, drinking and making out, and of the governor personally throwing them—some of them half dressed—out of her house. One shot showed her holding up her son's stash of weed.

Within twenty-four hours the photos were printed in a local newspaper with the headline TEENS GONE WILD AT ETON'S HOME. The underage drinking, illegal gambling and drug use started a political scandal and permanently damaged Mrs. Eton's reputation as governor. Coco and Spencer broke up, and Mrs. Eton packed her son off to military school. The gossip also prevented Spencer from getting into Yale—or any decent college, for that matter.

Word got around school that Haley had narced on Spencer, and soon she was ostracized by everyone—including Coco, who dropped her as soon as it became clear that associating with Haley was equal to social death. Even the outcasts didn't trust her. She had no friends, and no one ever invited her to a party ever again.

One little phone call—that's all it took to start this disastrous chain of events. Perhaps there was a better way for Haley to handle the situation?

●　●　●

Hang your head and go back to page I.

ALL ABOUT AUDREY

Some days there's nothing more fun than keeping the boys at bay.

"*Hola,* Haley. Happy snow day!"

Mia was lounging stylishly on the couch in Whitney and Sasha's TV room. School was canceled, and Haley had gone to the Klein-Lewis house to spend the day off watching movies with the girls.

"*Hola,* Mia," Haley said. "It's good to see you looking so . . . relaxed."

"I am relaxed, thanks to you," Mia said. "And your help with my leetle *problema.*"

"So no more Philip Fogelman?" Sasha asked.

"He is vanished from my life," Mia said. "Your mother's legal letter scared him off for good, Haley. Please tell her thank you for me. And thanks to the three of you, too, for being such loyal friends."

"I'm so relieved all that video craziness is over," Whitney said. Principal Crum, of all people, had gotten to the bottom of the mystery of the Hillsdale Hauntings Web site. He found out that the Troll, a classmate of Haley's who worked at a video-transfer shop, was the lamebrain behind most of the racy video postings. He'd even been paid off by Philip to include the Mia footage on the site. Principal Crum closed it down for good and suspended the Troll from school.

"I'm glad no one will watch me go 'boob tubing' ever again," Haley said. "And if I never see another inner tube it will be too soon."

"Let's forget all about that terrible episode in our lives," Sasha said. "Today we're going to watch good movies. I rented every Audrey Hepburn flick in the store. We'll start with *Roman Holiday,* then *War and Peace, Sabrina, Funny Face, My Fair Lady*—"

"People always tell me I look like Audrey Hepburn," Mia said.

Sasha laughed. "Mia, you're beautiful, and you're a brunette, but sorry, you look nothing like Audrey Hepburn. Even you aren't that pretty."

Mia looked stunned for a second. She obviously wasn't used to having her looks disparaged. But then she smiled. "Ha," she said. "I always thought so too—I don't look like her at all! But people said it, so I thought it must be true."

"I wish I had Audrey's accent," Whitney said. "You know, kind of British, kind of American, kind of something else?"

"I wish I had a perfect American accent," Mia said. "So everyone would not know right away I am Spanish."

"But your accent's sexy," Sasha said. "It drives the boys wild."

"No, I think I sound more sexy when I espeak Espanish."

"Girls, hot cocoa's ready!" Mrs. Klein called from the kitchen.

The girls trooped upstairs to get their mugs of cocoa. Whitney's mother, Linda Klein, and Sasha's father, Jonathan Lewis, were making latkes for Hanukkah. Mr. Lewis reached for one and Mrs. Klein playfully slapped his hand away. "No tasting yet!" she said.

"Can I just try them?" Mr. Lewis said, and kissed her quickly on the lips.

To Haley's surprise, Whitney and Sasha took this public display of affection in stride. They didn't seem to be grossed out by it at all. *They must be so used to it by now,* Haley thought.

"Sasha and Whitney, how would you like to light the menorah together tonight?" Mrs. Klein asked

"Sounds good, Mom," Whitney said. "After the first leg of the movie marathon."

The girls took their cocoa back to the TV room and settled in for *Roman Holiday*.

"Wow, the menorah?" Haley asked.

"I get to celebrate two holidays now," Sasha explained. "Hanukkah and Christmas. By the way, my mom's having a party at her house on Christmas Eve—I hope you're all coming. She's making crepes and she hired a jazz trio to play live."

"We can meet here first, if you want," Whitney said. "I've got fabulous presents to give all my BFFs before the party. And that includes all of you."

"Even me, Whitney?" Mia said.

"Um, sure," Whitney said. She'd come a long way, from despising Mia and thinking she was having an affair with her father to letting her into her little circle of friends. "Girls have to stick together. Besides, I want you to model for my spring campaign. My clothes will look amazing on you."

● ● ●

So, now that all the scandal has died down, another side of Mia appears. She may be a little spoiled by the constant attention her supermodel looks bring her, but it seems she's actually pretty nice underneath. Maybe even a new friend for Haley.

Now Haley has to cement her holiday plans. So many parties, so many choices! If you're positive Haley will not miss a night of live jazz and Christmas Eve festivities at Sasha's mom's cozy bungalow, turn to page **306, UNDER THE MISTLETOE.** If you think Haley wants to stick around her neighborhood and hang with Reese, turn to page **311, HIGH HOLIDAY.** To find out what Coco's up to on Christmas Eve, turn to page **301, HOME ALONE.**

LET IT SNOW

**When life hands you snow,
make snow angels.**

Haley woke up to a foot of snow. Downstairs in the kitchen her father was stirring a pot of oatmeal, and Mitchell spoke the magic words: "School's closed today."

"Awesome!" Haley said.

"What are you two going to do?" her mother asked.

Haley knew that some of her friends were planning on getting together at various houses for snow-day parties if school was indeed canceled, but she didn't feel like driving around town on slippery roads—and she knew her parents wouldn't be keen on the idea either. "I don't know," she said. "Want to build a snowman, Mitchell?"

"I want to build a snowman *army*."

They finished their breakfast, bundled up and went outside to play. Haley showed Mitchell how to make a giant snowball by rolling it around on the lawn. Soon they finished their first of many snow creatures. Mitchell put an old, loud tie of Perry's around its neck and declared it to be Merv Griffin.

"Is this a private party or can anyone play?" Reese hobbled over from next door dressed in ski clothes, with a black plastic garbage bag taped over his cast to keep it dry.

"We're making an army," Mitchell said.

"An army of seventies talk-show hosts," Haley added. "It's good to see you out and about."

"No cast is going to keep me from enjoying a snow day," Reese said. He patted a snowball together and tossed it at Haley. "But no fair playing rough."

Haley dodged the snowball and laughed. "Watch it, Highland. You can't get far with that cast on. If you're not careful you'll be buried up to your neck in snow."

"Yeah," Mitchell said. "And your head can be the snowman's head!"

"Oh no you don't," Reese said. "Besides, you

need my mad snowman-building skills to finish your army."

A group of elementary school boys trudged down the snowy sidewalk towing sleds. "Hey, Josh!" Reese called. "Get over here! We need your help!"

Josh and the other boys dropped their sleds and ran over. "They look about your age, Mitchell," Haley said. Mitchell hadn't made many friends in the neighborhood yet. He hung back shyly at first, but Haley knew he was excited to meet the other boys.

Haley showed them all how to make snow angels, and together she and Reese helped them pack up a supply of snowballs for a good long battle. Then they let the kids go at it.

"Looks like Mitchell has made some new friends," Reese said.

Haley nodded, thinking how sweet it was of Reese to be so nice to her little brother. "Thanks for your help. So, what are your plans for the holiday?"

"Not sure," Reese said. "Sasha's party sounds like fun, but my parents are going out on Christmas Eve, so it might be nice to stay home that night—if I had the right company, of course."

● ● ●

Reese can be a real doll when he wants to. Taking time off from sports seems to have brought out the best in him—and Haley is thrilled. The way he's taken Mitchell

under his wing is so sweet! As boyfriend material he's pretty hard to beat—or is he? If you think Haley's sure she wants to spend the rest of the holiday alone with her adorable next door neighbor, go to page 311, HIGH HOLIDAY.

On the other hand, she's not married to the guy. If you think Haley would like to mix it up a bit and have a GIFT SWAP with Alex Martin instead, turn to page 287. Finally, if you think Haley would rather spend the holiday with her friends at Sasha's mother's festive Christmas Eve party, complete with crepes and a jazz trio, go UNDER THE MISTLETOE on page 306.

Great minds think alike.

"Merry Christmas, Haley!" Annie Armstrong greeted Haley at the door of her house with a hug and a cup of homemade eggnog. She'd invited some friends over for Christmas Eve while her parents were out at a party. "Come in, come in," Annie said. "I've got to take the sugar cookies out of the oven."

Haley found Alex and Dave in the kitchen, munching on Annie's first batch of cookies. "Merry Christmas, everyone!"

"Merry Christmas," Alex said, kissing Haley on the cheek.

"I wish it were actually Christmas Day," Annie said. "My parents don't believe in opening presents on Christmas Eve like some families do, but I'm dying to know what they're giving me. I've got a feeling it's something special. Mom told me not to look in the garage while they're gone, so I know my present's out there. I'm dying to go and take a peek—"

"Annie, just let it be a surprise," Haley said. "Don't spoil your parents' fun."

Dave shook his head. "She's so impatient. She can't wait twelve little hours. . . ."

"It's true! I can't stop myself." Annie walked slowly toward the door that led from the kitchen to the garage. "Just a tiny peek." She opened the door a crack and peered into the dark garage. Then she slammed the door shut, screaming, "Oh my God! Oh my God! I don't believe it! It's too amazing to be true!"

"What is it?" Haley asked.

"Look for yourself," Annie said.

Haley opened the door. Parked next to Mr. Armstrong's sedan was an electric two-seater car with a giant red bow on top.

"Wow!" Haley cried. "They bought you an electric car!"

"I know! I know! I know! Can you believe it? I'm freaking out, I'm so excited!"

"Calm down, Annie," Haley said. "You're going to have to hide your excitement when your parents come home."

"And it's not like you can drive it yet," Alex said. "You haven't passed the driving test."

Annie gave Alex a dirty look. "I know, I know, but now I'll have to practice really really hard and re-take the test right away! Wow! A new car for Christmas!"

Dave stared at the car, then reached for a carrot stick. "That's really neat, Annie. Now you can drive me around."

"I can do whatever I want," Annie said. "I have a car!"

"Can I ask your advice about something?" Dave said, quickly losing interest in Annie's good fortune. "Do you think I should call my dad tonight and wish him a Merry Christmas?"

Haley exchanged a glance with Alex. They both had seen what had happened when Dave tried to visit his father: he'd chickened out. He couldn't even get up the nerve to introduce himself. Haley had no idea what Dave should do next, or even he was ready for a relationship with his paterfamilias. But, as usual, know-it-all Annie did.

"You absolutely should call him, Dave," Annie said. "Reach out to him. That's what Christmas is all about—family, and healing old wounds, and getting fabulous, fabulous cars!"

"I agree," Alex said. "Except for the part about the cars. Why not call him? What's the worst he can do?"

"Yell at me," Dave said. "Hang up on me. Tell me he's glad we're not a part of each other's lives."

"Well, would that really be so terrible?" Haley said, warming to the subject. "Then at least you'd know. Isn't it worth the risk of being hung up on? Besides, you might get a happy greeting from him instead."

"You can use my mom's study for privacy," Annie said. "I'm going to go sit behind the wheel of my new car. Just for a second."

Dave took his cell phone into the study and shut the door, while Annie ran into the garage to ogle her car some more. Which is how Alex and Haley suddenly found themselves alone in the kitchen. Haley ate a sugar cookie.

"Would you mind coming outside to my car with me?" Alex asked. "I've got a surprise for you."

"Sure." Haley grabbed her bag and went out to Alex's car. She had a surprise for him too.

Alex turned on the seat heaters and they sat quietly for a few minutes, listening to carols on the radio.

"I got you a little something," Alex said. He reached into the backseat and pulled out a copy of a magazine tied with a bow. "Merry Christmas."

Haley took the magazine. *The National Review.*

Wow. Thank you!" The headline on the cover said
A BOLD NEW YEAR FOR THE RIGHT WING. She started
laughing.

"What's so funny?" Alex said. "I got you a subscription. *The National Review* is a good conservative magazine, and I thought it would be nice
if you could understand my perspective on the is-
sues better. It could lead to some good, productive
debates. . . ."

Haley opened her bag and pulled out her gift for
him: a copy of *The Nation* tied with a bow, along
with a full year's subscription.

Alex grinned. "*The Nation*! The liberal bible!
That is funny. We're so in tune. I mean, about every-
ting except politics."

"I think you'll find some very interesting articles
in there about global warming," Haley said. "And
other favorite topics of mine."

"I'll be sure to read every issue," Alex said. "I
want to understand your point of view."

Haley felt as if she'd just seen a new side of
Alex—a less rigid side. Someone who really cared
about the world and about her. "For two people who
think so differently, we sure think alike."

Alex leaned toward her. "How about right now?
Are you thinking what I'm thinking at this very moment?"

Haley moved closer, slowly. "Yes," she whispered. "I think so."

He inched toward her until their lips touched in a sweet Christmas kiss. Alex was her opposite in many ways, but Haley thought maybe she'd finally met her match.

THE END

PRESENT TENSE

Don't get on the highway
of love unless you're ready
to heed the warning signs.

Haley's bag was heavy as she walked into Jack's Vintage Clothing on the afternoon of Christmas Eve. She'd spent the whole morning shopping for a gift for Devon, something really meaningful, and finally, in a used bookstore, she thought she'd found the perfect thing. It was an out-of-print collector's edition of a book by one of Devon's favorite photographers, Henri Cartier-Bresson. Haley bought it with the last of her babysitting money and had it gift-wrapped in metallic paper with a silver bow. Manly yet festive, she thought.

Devon worked part-time at Jack's, and she knew he had a shift that afternoon. Haley hoped it was the perfect time to give him the book and let him know how well she understood him and how much she liked him. If he had a present for her, too, that would seal the deal. *But* she wasn't expecting a gift in return. Mostly, she was hoping to move their odd, ambiguous friendship-with-romantic-vibes to the next level, in spite of Devon's recent especially standoffish behavior.

She took a deep breath and walked up to the counter. Devon was talking to a customer, a skinny guy in skinny jeans and high-tops with flipped-back seventies hair. Devon's eyes flicked toward Haley and registered her presence, but he didn't interrupt his speech to the customer.

"A skinny guy like you, if you really want the supertight jeans look, you've got to buy women's jeans," Devon was saying. "Just rip the label off and no one will know."

"Yeah, but I'll know," the guy said.

"You want the look, or you don't?" Devon said. "Joey Ramone wore chick jeans. You think he gave it a second thought? No. He didn't care what the label said, man. He cared about the look."

"Okay, okay, I'll try them on."

"Down that aisle all the way to the right," Devon

said. The customer went off in search of the women's jeans of his dreams. Haley stepped forward and presented Devon with her silver-wrapped gift.

"Hey," she said. "Merry Christmas."

"Hey," Devon said. "What's this?"

"Just a little Christmas present. Nothing big."

Instead of looking pleased, Devon looked annoyed. "I didn't have time to get you anything," he said defensively. "I've been real busy with work and everything."

"That's okay," Haley said. "I wasn't expecting anything. I just . . . saw this and thought of you."

Devon stared at the wrapped rectangle in front of him as if it might contain his mother's severed hand. "Open it," Haley said.

Reluctantly, Devon tore off the paper. He nodded with approval when he saw the book. "Cartier-Bresson. I really dig him." He flipped through the book and set it aside. Haley waited for him to say thank you, but he said nothing.

Now she didn't know what to do. Why oh why did she have to get him that present? How could she be so stupid? She felt totally awkward now. She didn't know what to say or do to make it better.

The door opened and Darcy pranced in. "Christmastime is here!" she sang. "Hi, Haley. Hi, Frosty." She playfully poked Devon in the stomach. "Did you burn that CD for me yet?"

"I've got it right here." Devon reached under the

counter, dug through his backpack and came up with a CD in a custom-made case covered with Devon's distinctive artful doodles. "I added a few songs I thought you'd appreciate."

"Cool. Thanks, dude." Darcy took the CD and dropped it into her own backpack. "See you back at the homestead, right? Later. Merry Xmas!"

Haley was speechless. Devon had no time to get anything for her, apparently because he was too busy burning a CD of songs chosen especially for Darcy. And drawing the cover himself. Something snapped inside her. Devon had sent her all the signals but she'd ignored them. Haley knew she'd been both a patsy and a fool. But she wouldn't be anymore.

"You know what, Devon? I get it now. I finally get it. Things aren't happening between us the way I'd like them to and now I understand why." The words blasted out of her like steam that had been building up pressure in a radiator. "You don't want it. Whatever it is we've had between us, a flirtation or romantic friendship or whatever, you don't want it to go any further. And guess what? I'm fine with that. I'm totally fine with it. I just wish I'd known how you felt a little sooner. Like, oh, last year when we met."

He stared at her in surprise and didn't say a word. She turned and stormed out of the shop, letting the door slam behind her.

Walking home, she was surprised at how light she felt. Almost as if she was flying. It was like she'd been carrying a boulder on her back all this time and she'd finally let it go.

Hours later, cozy at home by the fireplace, Haley wrapped presents for her family. Telling Devon how she felt was the best thing she'd done in ages. She hadn't realized before how much energy she'd been wasting trying to figure out what he was thinking, what was going on with him, whether he liked her or not. She wouldn't need to focus on him anymore. Now that he was no longer cluttering up her thoughts, she could move on to the next adventure.

She looked around at her warm and happy home, festively decorated for Christmas, and smiled, putting the wrapped presents under the tree. She couldn't wait to give them to Mitchell and her parents in the morning. *Boys may come and boys may go,* she thought, *but I'm so lucky to have friends, and a cool family. That's the most important thing.*

She'd be just fine without Devon McKnight.

THE END

UP FOR GRABS

**There's more than one way
to lose your shirt.**

"**C**ome on in and get warm," Matt said, leading
Haley inside his house and down the stairs to the
basement. Haley found herself in the laundry room,
leaning against a washer and dryer.

"Take off your jacket," Matt said. Haley obeyed,
and Matt touched the waffle shirt she wore underneath her fleece. "You're soaking wet."

"And freezing," Haley added.

"I'll get you fixed up," Matt said. "Take off your

wet layers and I'll throw them into the dryer. They'll be ready in ten minutes, and in the meantime I'll go upstairs and get you a towel. I'd hate to see you get sick."

Makes sense, Haley thought. She was shivering, and she didn't want to go home early just because her clothes were wet. It seemed so wimpy.

Matt leaned in and kissed her on the mouth. Before she knew what was happening he pulled off her wet shirts and tossed them into the dryer. Then he kissed her again. Haley shivered in just her bra and snow pants. "Please," she said. "It's cold in here."

"I'll be right back with that towel," Matt said. "Don't move." He turned on the dryer and ran upstairs.

Haley wrapped her arms around her body and looked for a blanket or something to cover herself with. She heard footsteps and thought it was Matt returning with the towel.

"Matt?" she said, peering up the stairs.

"Matt?" Spencer mocked, laughing. He came halfway down the stairs with Todd, Max and Jake. They all gaped at her in her bra. Haley hugged herself tighter.

"Going snow boob tubing this winter, Miller? I have to say, you really have developed nicely since that video."

Spencer and his friends cracked up. Haley

wanted to crawl into the dryer and die. *How did I get myself into this situation?* she wondered. *Why did I let Matt take off my shirt? Why do I keep trusting him? When am I going to learn?*

Good question. Hang your head and go back to page 1.

You can't trust a girl who isn't honest with herself.

Coco De Clerq pulled her hair into an updo and secured it with a jeweled barrette while Haley sat on the canopied bed and watched. "Have you been to Simone's before?" Coco asked. "No? You're going to *love* it! The food's fantastic, kind of French-Moroccan, and they have these tables with little lamps on them like in an old movie, and tonight they're having a band and dancing after dinner. I can't wait until Matt and Spencer get here." She checked her diamond-encrusted watch. "What's taking them so long?"

Haley smoothed her pale gold dress in the mirror, hoping she was glammed up enough for the fabulous night Coco had promised. A Christmas Eve double date with Coco, Spencer and Matt Graham. Coco had practically begged Haley to come, but Haley hadn't needed that much coaxing to have a fancy night out with a very cute guy.

Coco perched in front of her vanity mirror, applying coral lipstick. "I think I've been too hard on Spencer lately," she said. "You know, sometimes I have to remind myself that we're only in high school, and he's only seventeen. I feel so much more mature than that, but he's a guy, and you know how guys are—they mature way slower than we do."

Haley nodded, intrigued. This was a side of Coco she rarely saw: intimate, confessional, thoughtful. She liked it, for as long as it lasted.

"My New Year's resolution is to be more spontaneous," Coco said. "Less controlling. Just let the relationship happen, go with the flow, let it take me where it takes me."

Haley had to stifle a laugh. She appreciated Coco's confidence, but she couldn't imagine La De Clerq going with the flow unless she was possessed by the ghost of a flower child.

Coco checked her watch again. "They're almost an hour late! What's up with them?" She picked up her cell and speed-dialed Spencer for the third time since Haley had arrived. "I got his voice mail again," Coco fumed. "Spencer, where are you? Haley's here and we're waiting. We both look stunning so hurry up and get here before some other boys sweep us off our feet. Ha ha."

She clicked off with a grimace. "It's Christmas Eve. If Spencer ruins this night I—I want to say I'll kill him, but that wouldn't be going with the flow, would it? Unless the flow is leading me toward a career as a murderess. And I'd like to avoid prison if possible."

"Well, you did say that being more spontaneous was your New Year's resolution," Haley reminded her. "And it's not the New Year yet."

"True." Coco sat stiffly in a chair, careful not to ruin her hair or makeup. She didn't look very comfortable. Haley lounged on the bed, bored. After another hour and several more calls to Spencer's voice mail, Coco had finally had enough.

"I'm calling him one last time," she said, dialing. "And if he doesn't pick up . . . Spencer, Haley and I have been waiting for two hours now. Where *are* you? If you don't call me back within the next five minutes I'm breaking up with you—I mean it!"

She clicked off and said to Haley, "He'll call back now. Sometimes all it takes is a threat or two."

Haley couldn't take much more of this. She ransacked her brain for excuses to leave: *My parents are going out and I have to watch my little brother . . . I think I'm getting sick—achoo! . . . My mother just called and said Santa won't come until I'm home in bed and fast asleep. . . .*

Coco's cell rang. "That's him." She snapped it open. "Spencer, finally! What? I can't hear you over all that noise . . . What? Sasha's party? Spencer, how could you? I don't care if it's raging, you promised me. . . . Get over here right now! No, not 'much later,' I said now! Spencer, it's Christmas Eve. . . . How can you leave me alone like this? Yes, Haley's here, that's not what I meant. . . . Spencer!"

Coco looked grim, but she plastered a smile on her face as she hung up. "They stopped by Sasha's mom's party on their way over. They said it's a huge bore and they'll be here any minute."

" 'A huge bore'?" Haley said. "That's not how it sounded while you were talking. It sounded like he said they'd be here 'much later.' "

"He said that at first but I talked him into leaving right now," Coco said with false brightness in her voice.

"I don't think I can wait," Haley said. "I've got to get home—"

"Oh no you don't." Coco gripped Haley's arm, desperation in her eyes. "My parents are out, my sister's away, even Consuela is off tonight. You're not going anywhere until Spencer gets here. I can't be alone on Christmas Eve."

"But Coco—my parents—"

Coco refused to hear any excuse. "Besides, we'll have fun! Let's put on some music. We can dance, just the two of us. . . ."

Haley sighed while Coco frantically rushed around the room, looking for some way to entertain them. She'd made a mistake, trusting Coco. She should have gone to Sasha's party and skipped the date. Apparently everyone else had. Now she was stuck here with Coco, waiting for two boys who weren't going to show up for hours, if at all. Not exactly Haley's vision of the ideal Christmas Eve.

Next time, Haley vowed, *I won't let Coco pressure me into doing what she wants. Next time I'll do what I want to do and hang out with my friends.*

But for now she was stuck in an empty McMansion keeping a lonely girl company.

THE END

UNDER THE MISTLETOE

**Warm, happy Christmas
parties make kisses taste
all the better.**

"Bonsoir! Joyeux Noël!" Sasha's mother kissed Haley
on both cheeks as soon as she walked into the pretty
little bungalow, all lit up for Christmas Eve. The
house smelled wonderful, like pine and cinnamon
and cloves, and the party was already in full swing.
The fireplace was roaring, a jazz trio played softly in
the corner of the living room, candelabras glowed
with light and a long table groaned under platters of
European delicacies.

"Merry Christmas, Mrs. Lewis." Haley gave her a

bottle of sparkling cider as Sasha, Cecily and Whitney filed in behind her. The girls had stopped at Whitney's house on the way to the party because Whitney had promised them special presents—WK party dresses handmade by Whitney herself. Each girl received a beautiful sequined cocktail dress in a different color: gold for Sasha, silver for Cecily, green for Haley. Whitney had made a red one for herself. They were so fabulous, the girls all decided to wear their new dresses to the party that night.

"Please, call me Pascale," Mrs. Lewis said, taking their coats. "Well, don't you all look gorgeous! Whitney, you're a genius!"

Whitney smiled. "Thanks, Pascale."

"Please, come in, come in, have something to eat!"

Reese, Johnny and Drew were already there, munching on cheese and pate and bûche de Noël. "Wow," Reese said. "You girls look awesome." He caught Haley's eye, and she knew he thought she looked best of all.

"Yeah, you girls sure clean up good," Johnny Lane said, kissing Sasha. "And you smell good too. Almost good enough to eat."

"Would you like some punch?" Reese ladled punch from a crystal bowl into delicate glasses for the girls.

"Thanks," Haley said. More guests were arriving—chic-looking adult friends of Pascale's, classmates and friends of Sasha's. Even Spencer Eton and Matt

Graham showed up, and on the early side, too, for them. Clearly, Sasha's party was the place to be on Christmas Eve. Haley was so glad she'd come. She and Reese had fun tasting all the French delicacies, and with Sasha, Cecily and Whitney all in their special dresses she felt as though she was part of the coolest group of girls at school. And Coco was nowhere in sight.

Haley spotted Spencer pouring something from his flask into the punch bowl, and switched to eggnog. He was already slurring his words slightly.

"Haley, your dress is pretty, pretty." He touched the sequined fabric and Haley knew for sure he was drunk. "Sparkly. I like it."

"Thanks."

His cell phone rang, but instead of answering it he scowled at it. "That's just Coco again. She's driving me crazy. She won't leave me alone for a second! She's so controlling, you know?"

Haley wasn't sure what to say. She really wasn't in the mood to play relationship counselor to Spencer that night.

"She acts like my mother," he said. "I couldn't even tell her I was coming to this party tonight, 'cause she would have told me I couldn't. She would have forbidden me to come. Can you believe that? Who is she to tell me what to do? And now she's calling me every five minutes asking where I am and when I'm coming over to her boring house to go out to some boring-ass dinner. . . ."

"That's a shame." Haley tried to care, she really did, but what could she say? She didn't think it was right to talk about Coco behind her back, even if she sometimes deserved it, and besides, Spencer clearly wouldn't remember any of this in the morning, anyway.

Haley helped herself to another cup of eggnog. By midnight she started feeling a little fuzzy. She sniffed her cup and realized the eggnog had been spiked too—by Spencer, no doubt. She spotted Reese in the kitchen eating Nutella crepes with Cecily and Sasha. *Mmmm,* Nutella crepes . . . That was just what she needed. She started to make her way through the throng of partygoers to the kitchen, then stopped in the doorway and glanced up. *Hey,* she thought, *what's that green leafy thing hanging over my head?*

Just then Matt Graham grabbed her and planted a long Christmas kiss right on her lips. He tasted like rum and chocolate.

Stunned, Haley blinked at him. "What was that for?"

"Mistletoe." Matt nodded at the green leafy thing over their heads. "I saw my chance and I grabbed it."

Haley smiled. She felt swoony from that kiss. She'd never admit it, but Matt was a much better kisser than she'd expected. And it was a lovely way to end a perfect Christmas Eve. Except that Reese was now staring at her, looking jealous. Haley didn't take Matt's kiss too seriously—she wanted to keep things light that night. She was having too much fun hanging out with her friends and being free to worry about some silly boy.

THE END

HIGH HOLIDAY

Holidays are best spent
close to home.

"Your tree is so beautiful," Haley said. "And the presents are so perfectly wrapped. You should see the train wrecks under our tree. Mitchell likes to wrap his presents himself."

"My mother's kind of a perfectionist when it comes to wrapping." Reese handed Haley a mug of hot cocoa. He'd invited her over to spend Christmas Eve at his house. His parents were out at a work party and going to midnight Mass afterward, so

Reese and Haley had the house to themselves until at least one a.m. It was only nine o'clock now.

They sat on the couch in front of a roaring fire. The mantel was trimmed with evergreen boughs and the Highland family stockings. Reese propped his broken foot on a pillow. "I'm supposed to keep it elevated," he explained.

"That's cool," Haley said. She didn't mind his cast at all. It had forced Reese to slow down and pay more attention to her, and she was enjoying every minute of it.

"I hope you like a quiet Christmas Eve," Reese said, scooting closer to Haley. "I just couldn't deal with the parties this year."

"I think this is the perfect Christmas." Haley leaned closer to him until their shoulders touched. The fire made her face warm. "The snow outside, the tree, the fire, everything . . ."

She turned to face him and his lips were right there, ready for her. He kissed her. She tasted cocoa on his tongue. He pulled her close and kissed her deeper. They started making out, but then her leg knocked against his cast.

"Oh! Are you okay? Did that hurt?" she asked, sitting up suddenly.

"No. No, it's fine," Reese said, but Haley thought she caught a flash of pain in his eyes.

He lay back against the pillows on the couch and pulled her close. "Listen," he said. "My cast makes doing much of anything kind of awkward. . . ."

Haley knew immediately what he meant. If they tried to make out, his cast would keep getting in the way, and that wasn't very romantic.

"So do you mind if we just lie here together in front of the fire?" he finished.

"Not at all." She snuggled against him and he held her tight. They talked for hours, enjoying the quiet, snowy night, until his parents came home and found them both asleep in front of the fire. It was the most romantic night before Christmas Haley could imagine. Except there wasn't all that much romance in the end. But she felt closer to Reese than ever before, and that was what was important, right?

THE END